Shamim Sarif recently directed the motion picture adaptation of I Can't Think Straight.

She is also the writer/director of the award-winning feature film, The World Unseen, which is based on her novel of the same name. The book of The World Unseen won the Pendleton May First Novel Award and a Betty Trask Award.

She is the author of a further novel, Despite the Falling Snow.

She lives in London with her partner Hanan and their two children.

Acclaim for The World Unseen novel

"It is an impressive debut. Sarif's story brings together the descriptive power of the novelist with the screenwriter's mastery of dialogue."
The Times

"I read The World Unseen at a gulp, so entrancing is it's style, so complete it's tale of love and betrayal, and so accurate it's depiction of the physical, social and political scene…"
Johannesburg Star – Book of the Week

"Sarif's elegant and understated debut eschews emotional fireworks, and offers an unusual insight into early apartheid . . . a novel that lives up to its title" *The Times - Play*

"In the tradition of Vikram Seth, Sarif throws down a literary gauntlet that very few writers will be able to pick and return with any conviction."
Pride

"A really wonderful book. Sarif's writing is delicate and confident and the characters are real and very believable."
Maggie O'Farrell, author, "After You'd Gone" and "My Lover's Lover"

"Highly original…this is a stylishly written work. Sarif is near faultless…"
India Weekly

"The characters shine with the beauty of Sarif's deceptively skilful prose which keeps your eyes skating along the narrative in sheer enjoyment. I read this book in two long sittings, unable to put it down." *Dyverse*

"If you only read one novel for the rest of the year, make it this one. Sarif is a new writer who deserves to win prizes."
Waterstones

Acclaim for Despite the Falling Snow

"Despite the Falling Snow by Shamim Sarif, one of our most outstanding young novelists, is my novel of the year: its delicate artistry and immense compass reaches back to the labyrinthine heart of Soviet Russia"
Stevie Davies, The Independent

"Sarif's thrilling new novel makes me think of the 'The English Patient' and 'The French Lieutenant's Woman'. Like those books, it has at its core an unforgettable love story. Yet Sarif also understands the human cost exacted by totalitarian systems. And she knows that the worst betrayals are those committed by the ones we love. Her novel is immensely powerful – and deeply moving."
Steve Yarbrough, author of The Oxygen Man

"A perfectly balanced novel of love and tragedy...brutally shocking. The beauty of the streets of Moscow, the bejewelled architecture of the metro stations, is all a majestic backdrop to a play of mistrust and deception, where friends, even the best of friends, can turn against each other in fear."
Waterstones Magazine

"This story is, quite literally, breathtaking." *The Good Book Guide*

Explores love and tragic loss with the pace of a thriller and a style that is gentle and flowing, a hypnotic combination that eases between the US and 1950s Moscow. . . . A pure delight, highly recommended.
The Bookseller

An intriguing story of love, betrayal, anguish and despair . . . Shamim Sarif brings her characters to life with a delicacy of touch evocative of the intensity of their passions. An enthralling read." *Daily Dispatch*

"A compelling read, flicking expertly between the tragic present and tumultuous past...Haunting at times, Shamim's elegant prose weaves a poignant tale indeed." *Crush Books*

"Shamim Sarif's intense and elegant first novel drew on her South African roots. This one shows that her cultural compass can stretch even wider without dulling the delicacy of her gaze....Highly readable."
The Independent

First edition published in the United Kingdom by Enlightenment
Productions, London, UK, 2008
This edition published in the United States by Enlightenment
Press, 2009
www.enlightenment-press.com

ISBN Number: 978-0-9560316-1-7

I Can't Think Straight
Shamim Sarif

enlightenment

Acknowledgements

I made a trip to Amman to do some background research for this book a few years back now and remain grateful for all the help and information given to me by so many people. Amongst those who gave generously of their time, energy and contacts were Rania Atallah and Abdullah Said who arranged meetings and a visit to a refugee camp. My sister-in-law Maha Kattan and Zina Haj Hasan filled in a lot of detail about the customs and viewpoints of the region. Zein Naber, the most supportive aunt I could wish for, and her daughter Nadine, were also so generous with introducing me to people and showing us around their world in Jordan. Marwan Muasher, then Foreign Minister, took time from a busy schedule to meet with me and speak candidly and eloquently about his hopes and fears for the Middle East.

I worked on the screenplay of 'I Can't Think Straight' with Kelly Moss, who has been more than a friend in her support and belief in my abilities over the past few years. While the novel differs from the film in many ways, I have managed to shamelessly appropriate some of the best lines that Kelly wrote for the film and use them in this book, and I know she gives these lines willingly and without any cost to me, except the occasional long, liquid lunch.

Lea Porter was foremost amongst those friends of ours who encouraged me to write this story in the first place, and the 'no carbs' line is from her, as I confess I had no idea that anyone would willingly give up such a delicious food group!

I thank my family for their continuing support, and a special mention to my sister Anouchka who has always had unfailing faith in me, which I hope I can live up to.

Francine Brody edited this book with great delicacy but also great incisiveness that lifted many aspects of the story and it was a pleasure to work with her. My thanks also to Kirsty Dunseath for introducing us.

And last on this page, but always first in my thoughts, I thank Hanan, my wife, my inspiration and my greatest support. This particular story would not exist without her, and on a more fundamental level, none of my stories or films would exist either. With love and gratitude for all that you have given me.

For Hanan, the love of my life, who taught me that truth could be stranger than fiction, and much more beautiful.

And for Ethan and Luca, my loves, my life.

Chapter One

Amman, Jordan

A ND THEN THERE was the question of getting dressed, and time was running dangerously short. Reema could hardly spend this last hour before her daughter's engagement party arguing with Halawani about the cake. It was evident from the bulging smear of gold icing that was still slipping down the fabric-draped wall of the vast entrance courtyard that it was her own idiotic staff who had damaged it, probably Rani, wanting to be in charge of the fragile tower of soft sponge and peaked icing, and instead staggering into the wall under its unexpected weight. What did Halawani bake his cakes with anyway, to get that heaviness? As though the more sub-stance and solidity the thing had the better. It crossed her mind that perhaps she should have ordered it sent from London or, better yet, Paris. But if Reema was to be honest with herself (which she had spent a lifetime successfully avoiding, since honest appraisal of one's motives only caused more trouble than she had energy or inclina-tion to deal with) she had not felt her daughter deserved it. Not for the fourth engagement. Three previous French sponges had already been sent for, admired and eaten, and then she had been forced to

11

taste the bitterness of their regurgitation in her mouth when the engagements had been called off. Although, this time, she was sure that the betrothal would stick. This time, she was hopeful that at the age of twenty-eight, and despite two expensive, American degrees behind her, Tala had finally learned the most important lesson of life – that love and ideals were not actually real. Everyone loved the thought of them. Reema herself loved to read about them in books and watch them on television. But there was a reason why romance and passion were so suited to fiction; and to learn this lesson was a function of maturity, Reema thought, a growth away from the hotheadedness of youth. Over the last week, she had been pleased to see in her daughter's face a placid calm that was unfamiliar but most welcome. And yet a wriggling worm of tension curled inside her chest. The problem with Tala was that she always did what was least expected. And so if she did ruin this engagement, if it didn't last, Reema's one, poor consolation would be that she hadn't wasted money on the cake.

With only the slightest flinch, Tala had watched her engagement cake crash into the wall. She stood on the landing above, leaning silently over the banister rail, still and unnoticed, watching the flurry of movement in the hallway below. In the midst of the preparations, her mother and the baker were arguing over the smashed cake. She watched them both, body movements and gestures set against each other, heard their rising voices, irritated, pleading. Quickly, Tala turned and went back into her own room. She closed the door with finality by leaning her back fully against it and stood for a moment as if casting around for something to hold onto. Her eyes went to her desk, her laptop, her work. She sat down to finish correcting a contract that had been sent to her earlier that day. The soft shift of her pencil on the stiff paper soothed her in some way, until the chime of her mobile interrupted her. She answered it, while her pencil continued to work.

'We could just elope, you know.'

She smiled at Hani's voice.

'But then you wouldn't get to see me dressed like a Bond girl,' she replied dryly. He laughed.

'Must be insanity over there. With the preparations and everything?'

Tala had just found three errors in one clause and neglected to answer quickly enough.

'Tala? You're working aren't you? Half an hour before our engagement party starts!'

Tala laid the proofs on the desk and leaned forward in her chair. 'It's my first order, Hani. I have to make it work. My father's already pressing me to come back to the family business.'

'You will make it work,' he replied, his voice serious, kind. 'You will. I love you, Tala.'

Tala smiled at the phone. 'Me too, Hani. Me too.'

When he rung off, she did not pick up her work again, but sat still for a moment, the kind of pause she rarely allowed to punctuate her days. There was music outside floating up to her from the garden – the band was testing microphones and speakers. Closing her eyes, she frowned, straining to hear the song that was being sung. Heartbreak and sorrow seemed enveloped in the soft liquidity of a female voice, which had an underlying richness that poured along the registers of notes like warm syrup. Her cadences and inflections, the heart-stopping pause as she sang up or down a range, were uniquely Eastern, unmistakably Arab. But the voice was buoyed from beneath by the flamenco rhythms of a guitar and it was pulled higher by the intense, aching stretch of two violins. She listened for a few seconds more, until the band halted their test abruptly, and then she returned, with concentration, to her contract.

Reema glanced at the kitchen clock. For fifteen minutes now, she had been trying to get Halawani to take back the cake and repair it, which he steadfastly refused to do lest she interpret it as an admission of guilt on his part (which of course, she would have). Turning on her velvet-slippered heel, she left the competing protestations of the staff and the baker, not to mention the grating screech of the microphones that were being tested outside, and the irritating itch of her husband's nervousness as he watched two hundred table settings of silver and stiff linen being checked, and stalked across the heavy blocks of pure marble that covered the entire ground floor of the house like the finely veined, flawless skin of a soft-complexioned woman. She stepped carefully onto the wide sweep of the staircase and walked up as if leaving a room filled with a hundred admirers. It was one of her small pleasures, this ascending of the staircase, which was such a showpiece, such a piece of theatre, suspended above the flowing expanse of the living area below. At the top she turned left (the right wing of the house contained her daughters' suites) and crossed twenty yards of hallway before gaining her own bedroom. The bed was of gargantuan proportions, adorned with a selection of suede and silk cushions. She liked the romance of the look, and it was echoed in the hand-painted wallpaper, in the florid flounce of the curtains and in the plump pinkness of the sofas which framed the sitting area. Conscious of the time, Reema walked straight into her dressing room, where the much-anticipated pleasure of a strong cigarette awaited her.

Her Indian housekeeper, Rani, was standing in the middle of the room, holding two glittering evening gowns, each arm stretched high above her head in an effort to prevent the hems from touching the carpet. She was only barely successful in her endeavour, since she was a good eight inches shorter than Reema and her dresses.

Reema paused and her eyes flickered intently over each gown. She pointed. 'That one.'

'Yes, Madam'.

With relief, Rani laid down the gowns. The tops of her arms ached.

'Where's my coffee?'

'Coming, Madam.'

Reema sat upon the plush, velvet chair before the towering, three-panelled mirror, attached a slim black holder to the end of the cigarette, applied the flame of an alabaster lighter to the other end, and sat back. Her face was not bad, she considered. Not for a fifty-four year old mother of three. She sighed out a cloud of cigarette smoke. She was aware that the continuous dragging on cigarettes had deepened the lines around her eyes and mouth, but they were not as bad as those of the other women in her bridge group (except for Dina, but everyone knew she had a Brazilian plastic surgeon practically on her payroll).

Rani re-appeared carrying a pot of Arabic coffee and a small silver cup. She placed these on the table behind Reema, poured out a cupful of the steaming dark liquid and, with a sidelong glance at Reema's unsuspecting back, silently spat into it.

'Your coffee, madam.' Rani crossed the room and politely offered the cup to Reema. She watched eagerly as Reema lifted the coffee to her lips, but only to blow a cooling breath onto it.

'Where's my husband?'

'In the garden, madam.'

'Did the dress fit Tala?' Reema asked. 'She didn't stop eating at lunch.'

'Like a glove, madam.' Rani watched the coffee cup's movement up and down, the gentle cooling of the liquid. Let her drink it, she prayed. Let her drink it.

'Lamia – did you take in her clothes?'

Rani nodded. 'By two centimetres, madam.'

Satisfied, Reema lifted the coffee to drink but then remembered her youngest child. Rani shifted a little.

'Did Zina like the gold dress I chose for her?' The cup touched Reema's lips, was tipped up ready for the first sip.

'She loved it, Madam.' Rani's careful tone was designed to smooth over the sarcasm of the reply, but only caused Reema to lower the coffee cup and throw her housekeeper an evaluating stare. Rani smiled brightly, encouragingly, but it was too late. Reema placed the untouched coffee back into her hands and began to apply her make up.

The moment that Zina had seen her sister's engagement cake, she had felt blindly impelled to get out of Jordan and back to New York. The teasing restlessness of her limbs, the impulsive desire to turn and walk calmly, coolly through the quiet house and out of the immense double front doors, was almost overwhelming. She pictured herself out there, outside, walking, walking on, picking up the rhythm of her stride as she made her way along the winding private road that led down their own private hill and towards the dark surroundings of the Jordanian countryside. Away to her right, she would see the lights of Amman, winking seductively from this distance; she would look up and see the startling white purity of the stars, studded into the ebony sky, guarded by a desert moon as sharp-edged as a scythe.

Zina sat up on her bed, disappointed – with herself, for wanting to escape Tala's party – but mainly with the cake. Until she had parted her curtains and watched the garish bulk of that cake being brought into the garden, she had been successfully convincing herself that she was glad to be home. Most of her apparent contentment had been achieved at her own expense, through basic psychological trickery. She knew she was adept at evoking a romantic nostalgia for things like the jasmine trees, the scent of smoked aubergines, even the ageing faces of her mother and father. But it was all a fantasy of the mind, an elaborate structure to enable her to get through an evening, a week, a month in this place, without succumbing to a nervous breakdown. Gold icing. Who, in God's name, ever used gold icing? It looked metallic, the cake, as though it had been sprayed with car paint and it encapsulated everything that irritated her about the Middle East. The gaudy, unnatural look of it, the probably poisonous taste of it.

And then there was the dress. Draped across the foot of the bed was an offensively gold concoction. Pinned to the shoulder of the dress was one of her mother's stiff, gilt-edged note cards. In Reema's florid hand were written the words: 'No black. It's an engagement party, not a funeral. Mama.' She could imagine her mother had congratulated herself for an hour after thinking up that hilarious line. Carelessly, Zina pulled the note off and tossed it into the bin. As she regarded the dress mournfully, it became clear to her (and not for the first time) that her mother obviously hated her. A tear of self-pity touched Zina's eye, even as she realised something far more serious – that her dress had obviously been chosen to match the cake. A snapshot of a previous engagement cake, an emerald-turreted confection – had it been Tala's first? – flashed into her mind, and beside it, her mother, somewhat younger, in a brilliant green Yves Saint Laurent dress and matching eyeshadow that had not seemed so inelegant amid the general style overkill of that period.

Drawing in a long breath, she tried to dispel the vague nausea that suddenly touched her, and made a conscious effort not to recall the other cakes, the other parties, the broken engagements, the desperate fiancés, the feuding families. In one short week she would be back at university in New York, and would have a month to recover from this trip before returning for the wedding. In the meantime, she began to list in her mind the things that would help her to get through the evening without resorting to sarcasm or sullen silence. At the top of that list was the knowledge that she would not be putting any of that cake into her mouth. If it was bad luck, then so be it. Frankly, she had eaten cake three times before, and not one of the engagements had stuck. Although, a moment later, the thought struck her that perhaps that had been the good luck after all. She smiled slightly and headed into the bathroom.

'Is this seven millimetres?'

Lamia, waiting for mirror space behind the broad shoulders of her husband, stepped forward and peered at the ruler that he used to measure how much of his handkerchief peeked from his tuxedo pocket. She nodded, and Kareem lowered the ruler and turned away, satisfied.

'I just hope this is the last engagement party your father has to throw for your sister.'

Lamia tried very hard to concentrate only on her own reflection in the polished glass. She adjusted her necklace, pleased with the way it set off the elegant sapphire-blue of her evening dress. But Kareem was fidgeting at his immaculately ordered closets, checking that the edges of his ties were aligned, needling the perfect rows of socks, needling her.

'Poor man,' he said, clicking his tongue.

'He doesn't mind,' Lamia offered.

'Of course he minds. He's kind enough not to show it. But for a man of his standing to endure the shame…'

Lamia closed her eyes just long enough to block out the sound of her husband's voice. She opened her eyes, and cast a half-smile at her own reflection before turning to him.

'How do I look?' she asked.

Kareem's long-lashed brown eyes passed over her figure and for a brief, pleasurable moment, Lamia felt conscious of her own beauty.

'You could cover your shoulders a little more.'

She looked down. 'It's not cold.'

He plucked a shawl from the closet and strode across the room, holding it out to her.

'It's not proper.'

The music, over which the first guests were chatting, still haunted Tala as she descended into the garden which was transformed for this night with hundreds of lamps and glowing lanterns that created an expansive circle of light around the crisply dressed tables and the open sided marquees. Beyond the lights were swathes of lush lawn (Reema had insisted on installing an impractical and hideously expensive state-of-the-art irrigation system to crush once and for all the relentlessly encroaching desert landscape) and dotted between were fountains, footpaths and the occasional piece of ancient sculpture, dramatically lit for the occasion. Tala paused in the shadows and looked around. There were softly translucent candles, and music that rose in ripples behind the tide of chattering voices. There were exquisite dresses cut from elegant fabrics, draped over long, slim bodies; there were jewels that gleamed against tanned, olive skin. There were butlers and waitresses, in starched white and rustling black, moving with purpose amongst the colourful women and the suited men. Tala knew that her parents had outdone themselves. She had been surprised that they had even suggested a party this time around, bearing in mind her dubious history, but it had become clear to her quite quickly that her mother was actively planning to use this fourth and final engagement as a way to wipe clean all the lingering shame and embarrassment of the other three. Reema had organised a party designed to scream her family's support for their eldest daughter, and to ensure that nobody missed the fact that this final fiancé outshone even the three wealthy heirs she had previously been promised to, because Hani was handsome and articulate, as well as Palestinian, Christian and rich. Tala lingered at the edge of the party, holding back from that first plunge in to people and talk and dancing, and looked around her, narrowing her eyes slightly, so that the deep, liquid blue of the sky, which held a crisp-edged moon and coldly bright stars, was rimmed at the lower edges with the flickering pulse of the candlelight.

Uncle Ramzi spotted Tala first, pulling his niece into a small circle of people. The women kissed her, commenting on the simple, clean lines of her dress in an effusive way that made her understand that they disliked it. The men grinned their congratulations. The young ones had carefully slicked hair and, like their fathers, held glasses of whiskey. Her uncle was already smoking a Montecristo cigar shaped like a small torpedo. Tala hugged him.

'Ammo Ramzi! You managed to get on a plane!'

Ramzi pulled back in dismay. 'Plane? You know I'll never get on a plane. Not after that dream I had.' His large hand mimed the sudden crash of an aircraft. He shook his head sorrowfully. 'The crash! The devastation!'

'Ammo, the dream was in 1967.'

'Right after the Six Day War,' agreed Ramzi. 'Israel has a lot to answer for.' This drew sympathetic murmurs from the people around them even as Ramzi assured her that he would not have missed her party for anything.

'I wanted to meet the man who made it this far – again.'

There was a flutter of laughter and Tala glanced up at the circle and caught the nervous expectation in the fading sounds they made. The last time she had broken an engagement, she had done so at the party itself, irritated beyond control by the insulting, chauvinistic bravado her fiancé had adopted in front of his family and friends. Despite her instinct to brush off their clinging curiosity with a joke, Tala felt lost suddenly. She looked to her father, instinctively, for some quiet support but he had moved away, always unable to stand still, and was directing several tuxedo-clad waiters to re-position the heat lamps around the immaculately laid tables. The night was cool, after a day that had been harshly hot, and the persistent breezes would only become colder as the night wore on. Then, at the far edges of the informal circle surrounding her, she caught sight of her youngest sister. Zina's eyes were fixed on her own with a serious look under which amusement lay bubbling. The touch of that glance restored her and she turned back to her uncle.

'I love him, Ammo.'

'Of course you love him. He's Christian and he's rich.'

'He's kind and honest and forward-thinking. And handsome,' she added, to soften the insolence that they would have perceived in her tone. Her uncle smiled, but leaned in to her as he accepted a glass of champagne from a waiter. Tala noticed Ramzi's eyes lingered appreciatively on the young man's form as he took the glass from him.

'Handsome is good, my dear. But ask your aunty why she married me. Looks and character come and go. Only large sums of money last forever.'

He was rewarded with guffaws from the men, and faux-disapproval from the women, most of whom, Tala noted, had married for money rather than love.

'Apparently so,' she replied, and they were uncertain of the meaning of this reply, and because they were uncertain they read it, correctly, as an insult, though none of them showed it. They only laughed outwardly and congratulated themselves inwardly that their own children were not as over-educated and smart-assed as Reema and Omar's.

Her duty done with her uncle, Tala extricated herself and found Zina.

'You look amazing, habibti,' her youngest sister told her.

'Thanks. I wish I could say the same,' Tala replied, taking in her sister's gold dress. Ruefully, Zina glanced down at herself.

'You know, I think I found those weapons of mass destruction the Americans were looking for. How clever to disguise them as Mama and Lamia. I wish you'd come from London earlier,' Zina added. 'Who shows up the night before their engagement?'

'I was working, Zina.' Tala's tone held the air of a confession. Zina squeezed her hand, a touch of encouragement and understanding. She felt better, calmer, reassured by the familiar exchanges with Tala. There were times when Zina regretted that for the past fifteen years she and Tala had lived in different countries. While Tala had finished boarding school in Switzerland, Zina had remained at home in Amman with her parents. By the time she followed Tala and Lamia to school, the two older girls were already at university. Perhaps she had been focusing on the wrong type of nostalgia this week.

'Are you excited about the wedding?' Zina asked. Tala shot her a sarcastic look.

'Flower arrangements, menus and napkin rings? I can't wait.'

Zina smiled. 'Then why are you getting married?' There was only a small hint of amusement in her eyes and in the tone of her question.

'What should Hani and I do?' Tala asked. 'Live together?'

'It's modern times.'

'Not in Amman. You've been in the States too long. These six months dating Hani are the longest I've ever gotten away with, without a ring.'

Zina considered. 'I think you should blaze a trail.'

'So it's easier for you and Lamia?' Tala laughed.

'Lamia?' Zina snorted. 'She's set us all back by a century.'

Instinctively, they both looked over at their sister, who caught their eyes upon her and made her way to them. She looked at Tala. 'Mama says you should be entertaining your guests.'

Zina laughed. 'Yeah, Tala, you really should be familiar with engagement party etiquette by now.'

'That's not funny,' Lamia noted.

Zina regarded Lamia with all the irritation that had built up since she had coerced her into putting on the heinous dress. 'It is if you possess a sense of humour.'

Tala sighed. Before them, the swimming pool glowed with submerged lighting and the interior walls displayed a delicate, intricate mosaic. The white-clothed tables radiated out from the pool over the lawns, while beyond, the wild profusion of jasmine trees and flowers stood sentinel, scenting the air with their perfume.

'Hani's here!' Lamia exclaimed.

They followed Lamia's gaze. At this distance, Hani was hard to pick out amongst the group of relatives who accompanied him, for he wore a similar tuxedo and hairstyle, and he seemed very much at ease amongst the back-slapping, shoulder-squeezing, loud congratulations that the men conferred on him as he arrived. But Tala noticed that he glanced up at every opportunity and she knew that he was looking for her; and when his eyes did find her own, their calm, even gaze reassured her.

'God, you're lucky, Tala,' Zina said.

'I know.'

She went forward to meet him, exulting in the familiar smell of his skin and clothes, clinging to him for a long hug. Only the smattering of applause from guests watching them brought her back to herself, to self-consciousness.

'Have you had a drink?' Hani asked her, holding her hand. Tala shook her head and he picked up two glasses from a passing tray.

'Here,' he said, smiling. 'To you and me. To us, Tala.'

She touched his glass with her own 'To us, Hani.' Tala grasped his hand and turned to listen to the girl who was singing. She was raised high on a special dais on the other side of the pool, far enough removed from the partygoers to appear like a lone angel spreading her message in vain. Tala listened, aware of only the music and the throb of her own rushing pulse in her ears, from a heart that she felt now as a physical presence in her chest, swelled with emotion; a spilling of feeling that she could not recognise as either happiness or sorrow.

Chapter Two

London

IT WAS HALF-PAST FOUR on a Friday afternoon — those revered and sacred minutes in a quiet, British suburban office, when the weekend had finally crept so close that the anticipation of it was pleasurable rather than agonising. Leyla looked forward to these two days hungrily, more excited by the prospect of release from her office, with its rain-flecked window and the grim brightness of its three fluorescent tubes, than by any particular plans. The low pall of the Surrey sky matched the relentlessly beige paint on the walls, which were not noticeably helped by the photographs and pictures that she had long ago hung on them. She took a sip of cooling tea and flicked open her notebook. A sentence had occurred to her as she had looked from the buzzing light tubes to the steely sky, and she wanted to get it down before she lost it. She did so, then carefully busied herself for a moment by closing the computer spreadsheet she had been working on, before she allowed herself to re-read the line. She nodded slightly, pleased. There was one good thing to be said for working with numbers all day – she could hardly keep up with the words that fought to spill out of her in the evenings.

During the last six months, she had almost completed a first novel, and she was surprised to find herself pleased with what she had produced. She had been daunted, at the start, by the sheer hubris of daring to put down on paper the sudden clusters of words that peppered her thoughts, and certainly she would not allow her mind the pleasure of imagining these snatched hours of writing, these short patches of consciousness detached from the regular, even shapes of the world about her, as a way of life that might one day come to fill all her days.

'Leaving early?' her father asked her with a grin. It was over an hour later, and he had caught sight of her trying to pass noiselessly through the open car park that his office overlooked. He did not care that his daily view consisted of two Mercedes, a Volvo, a Toyota and two Ford Fiestas; he liked to notice the flow of bodies in and out of the office. For Leyla, it seemed particularly harsh that, so close to Friday evening freedom, she should have heard the unmistakable, familiar tap on the window, and been forced to turn and walk back in to see him.

'Hardly early,' she said, with a quick smile. 'It's six. In fact you owe me an hour's overtime.'

Sam laughed. His office was large, with an impressive boardroom table that remained completely unused, for there was no board to report to, and a stained mahogany desk broad enough to complement his tall, solid frame. He sat back in his wide leather chair, laced his hands behind his head, and said, with calculated casualness:

'This is all going to belong to you and Yasmin one day, you know.'

It was a familiar lead-in, and she smiled even as she felt a misgiving hit her in the stomach.

'But it won't keep going without sales,' he continued.

'You know I'm no good at selling, Dad,' she began, but her manner was too hesitant, her pitch too half-hearted. She hated to say things that disappointed him and, as a result, she realised that she couldn't even sell him the idea that she was not a salesperson.

'You don't sell life insurance,' her father assured her.

'I know, I know,' she replied. 'It sells itself.'

'Exactly,' he smiled, pointing a finger at her. He was charming, she had to admit that.

'Life insurance,' he continued, 'is a sure bet. We all know we're going to die.'

She placed her notepad, briefcase and coat down in a heap on the floor. She had been clutching them against her as a kind of talisman, in the hope that he would be psychologically fooled into thinking that she was in a hurry to get home. But now there was no denying the truth – a full day pinned behind his desk, dealing with the paperwork he so disliked had left him thirsty for human contact, hungry for an audience. With relief, she remembered that she had an unbeatable way out, but he was so happily animated that she could not bear to play her card just yet.

'You think I like selling? I've got news for you – I don't.'

That was a blatant lie if ever she'd heard one. He loved selling. He lived and died for it; and he did it superbly. He sold things all the time, even at home. He would delight in asking if she and her sister wanted their chicken curry with chapattis or rice – thereby ensuring that they accepted the curry itself without argument. It was the law of limited choices, he would explain. Never ask a potential client if he'd like to see you; ask him which time would be better for him. The psychology of it was interesting, but on the rare occasions she had tried the strategy, even to pin down errant photocopier repair men, it had not worked. 'Would morning or afternoon be better for you today?' she would gamely ask, only to be told that the next available slot was for the following Thursday. She felt sure that knowing how to approach the client was only half the battle; that one must also possess bottomless reserves of resolve, confidence, chutzpah. She felt a surge of admiration pass through her, that her father had found within this industry a passion and drive that made him endlessly inventive in his sales techniques, constantly excited, and extremely successful.

'I don't sell anything,' he reiterated. 'I just ask my client if he's going to die? There's only one answer. Then, I ask him – are you one hundred and fifty per cent happy that your wife and kids are going to be taken care of the way you want them to be, for the entire rest of their lives?' He paused here, to recreate the dramatic tension of the moment. 'You know what? They always hesitate. And then,' he said, slapping his large fist into an equally capacious palm. 'You've got 'em.'

She cleared her throat. It certainly did not sound difficult. Only two questions – you knew there was no dodging the first one, and the second was a zinger too. She pictured herself sitting before a potential client, probably the son of a prosperous, suburban businessman who had been her father's client previously. They would be sitting in the drawing room, with cups of tea before them. There would have to be some small talk (another thing she was poorly skilled at). And then, she would have to make her pitch. She tried to do so, now, in her head, but all that stood out was the imagined client's shocked face when she told him with great force that he was definitely going to die. She pictured him: defensive, irritated, unhappy. She tried to move on to the next point, the main point, the part about his wife and children being taken care of, but could not. Her mind blanked, fully, utterly, and the chintz living room dropped out of her mind's eye, leaving her with a string of words. Gratefully she realised that she had located, without even looking for it, the opening sentence for her next chapter. She glanced involuntarily, longingly, at the notebook by her feet, then up at her father.

'Maybe I can keep the business going on the admin side,' she suggested. 'Like I'm doing now.'

'Administration is meaningless,' he replied. 'Unless there are sales. Sales bring in the money.'

He was right of course, and this afternoon's short course in the joys of salesmanship was part of a much broader, ongoing education entitled Taking Over The Business. Leyla's sister had already unceremoniously flunked this course when she had elected to spend two years after university working with an NGO in Kenya. Since her recent return she had resolutely refused Sam's offers to join the business, instead insisting on working for a caterer with a view to starting her own food supply company, having been inspired by two years of goat stew and boiled mealies never to be without access to gnocchi, lemongrass or salmon roe ever again. Their father was merely mortified that three years of International Relations at a top British university had left his younger daughter a waitress.

'I have a date with Ali this evening,' Leyla said, trying to cover her desperation with an air of casual recollection.

As she had anticipated, this sentence successfully derailed the sales recruitment drive. Her father raised his eyebrows.

'That's good. Where are you going?'

'Into town. We're visiting a friend of his, then dinner.'

'It's Friday, you know. Your mother and I will be at the mosque.'

'Dad, I believe in our religion. You know I do. I just don't like to go when everyone else does.' It was hard for her to push her point of view, and there were many areas in which she remained silent to avoid conflict, but in some, small aspects she knew she had to stand firm or be completely subsumed.

'If you don't go with everyone else, how will they know you're a good Muslim?'

She laughed, grateful for his gracious capitulation.

'Go on, then,' he told her. 'Don't be home too late.'

'I'm twenty three, Dad.'

He looked at her for a moment. 'I know,' he said, gently. She retrieved her coat and her keys and the precious notebook from the floor and then went to the door.

'I won't be late,' she told him and she left, with an ache of regret in the base of her stomach. Regret that she found it so disproportionately hard to live up to his reasonably pitched ideals, and regret that the brilliant sentence that had occurred to her a few moments before was now lost to her mind forever.

London, for Leyla, possessed a debonair glamour that was perhaps enhanced by only limited exposure to it when growing up in the shelter of its suburbs. In Ali's car, sleek and silver and low to the ground, they piloted through Hyde Park, towards Mayfair. The sun was setting now, had lowered so far that it had escaped the shield of cloud that had concealed it all day, and was spread like a molten slice of liquid gold over the tops of the trees. The curling, unfurling ribbons of cloud that extended on each side were touched with pink and red.

'Did you arrange that just for me?' she asked.

Ali looked out of her window. 'What?' he asked.

She pointed, hiding her surprise that he had not noticed the glow of light beyond the window. 'The sunset,' she said.

He looked again, then smiled. 'Oh yes. It's beautiful.'

They parked beneath a streetlamp that had just begun to glow yellow and walked past the grand facades of old buildings, gleaming in the soft dusk. Glimpses of other lives attracted her to the windows that they passed. There were high ceilings and sparkling lights; in one framed, brief tableau she saw two waiters setting a long table. In another, the soft glow of firelight played on two armchairs where newspapers were being read in a club.

'How do you know Tala?' Leyla asked as they walked.

'Her first fiancé was my best friend at university. I met Tala through him.'

'First fiancé? How many has she had?'

Ali grinned. 'She's currently on number four.'

'Four?!' There was a profligacy to this number, as it related to betrothals, that left Leyla momentarily breathless with surprise.

'He's a lovely guy, from Jordan. I think this one will stick. And then she'll spend more time in Jordan and less here in London. Her family has houses in both places.'

'So where does she work?' Leyla asked.

'She's always helped her father in the family businesses. But she's been trying to set up something of her own from London. Working with Palestinian suppliers. Her family is Palestinian, originally.'

'Refugees?' she asked, startled.

He laughed. 'I suppose all Palestinians are; but they were lucky. They had a business in Jordan before Palestine was lost, so they came out of it much better than most.'

They reached the front door of an imposing, white stuccoed house, and Ali rang the bell. Their eyes met as Leyla straightened the line of her blouse.

'What's the matter?' he asked. 'You nervous?'

She nodded and he touched her hand kindly.

'Tala's great. Trust me, you'll love her.'

It struck Leyla as strange that they had ostensibly come to visit Ali's friend Tala, but had so far met only her parents. She sat forward in her antique chair, attentive and polite, holding a fragile, miniature glass cup whose rim was delicately threaded with gold. The glass was filled with a sweet, amber tea in which an escaped mint leaf floated. Leyla sipped at it, watching the parents with interest, especially the mother, for after a week at work in the restrained, self-deprecating and often colourless atmosphere of an office in Surrey, Reema appeared to her to be somewhat exaggerated as a person. While Tala's father and Ali fell deep into a conversation about business, Reema inserted a cigarette into an improbably long holder and lit it with a miniature gold palm tree that erupted into flame. There followed a quiet moment in which Leyla sipped at her tea while Reema enjoyed in peace the first, deep inhalation of nicotine, before she turned her attention to her guest as she hissed a stream of pungent smoke into the room.

'So, how long have you and Ali been dating?'

Leyla hesitated. 'About two months.' In truth, the actual time had blurred into a larger block of her life that she could not immediately grasp hold of. Reema's appraising eyes flickered over Leyla.

'And? Does he want to marry you?'

Taken aback, she laughed. 'I don't know.'

In fact, she suspected that he was very much interested in marrying her. She had not gained this awareness from any deep issuing of emotion on his part, but because it was commonly understood amongst their friends and family and wider community, that Ali had decided to 'settle down'. And since she came from the same religious background as he, and since he had the advantage of money, business acumen and charm it would have been inconceivable for her to turn him down when he asked for a date. She herself hadn't thought it reasonable to say no without meeting him, although she was surprised that he had even asked her. She was not sociable, and lacked enthusiasm for more than occasional invitations out. She was fit (she ran most mornings, around the quiet sprawling roads that surrounded their house), and slim as a result, but shopping for clothes bored and confused her, and so she never had the perfect outfit for any given situation, but would make do with the few good pieces that she had, and which her sister Yasmin had helped her pick out. It had occurred to Leyla after Ali continued calling her that perhaps he found her general gaucheness artless and appealing in some way. For his part, he had proved intelligent, articulate and adept, eager to learn, well-travelled and generous. And after several weeks she was indifferent to him, except as a friend; in that capacity she was deeply attached to him. As far as she could ascertain, he might be happy to stride into a marriage on the basis of this friendship, whereas she could not. And they were still together because while she suspected all this to be true, she could not bring herself to be presumptuous enough to take his intentions for granted, and so she could not speak of the marriage issue until he did. For now, therefore, they remained good friends and Leyla studiously ignored the fact that, in her mind, they seemed to be steering in different directions.

'Tala's engagement party was last week in Jordan. The best party anyone had seen in Amman for some time,' Reema reminisced with a smile. 'Tala's the eldest. My middle one, Lamia, got married straight out of college. She's very beautiful, though.'

Leyla hesitated, unsure she had heard this last comment correctly, thereby giving Reema time to toss in another question.

'What does your father do?' Reema inhaled again, hungrily.

Footsteps were moving quickly down the hallway. Leyla had an instant mental picture of a rich, well-dressed Middle Eastern daughter with immaculate hair, nails and make-up, accessorised and high-heeled to within an inch of her life. Instead, a tall young woman in jeans strode in and shook her head at Reema.

'Stop interrogating the poor girl, Mama.'

Leyla stood up quickly, watching as Ali grasped Tala in a bear hug and when Tala turned to her, Leyla held out a hand, friendly but formal. Tala regarded the hand with an air of amusement before leaning to kiss the girl on both cheeks. Leyla smiled and reciprocated, not wanting to appear awkward, although she was. She had never learned how to decide when to offer a hand versus a kiss. Other people seemed to drift easily into the right method for the right person; there must be some intricate web of body language that Leyla had not grasped, or perhaps it was her innate reserve that held her back more easily than it urged her forward. Tala smiled, noting the indecision in Leyla's movement.

'Sorry to break your British reserve,' Tala said. 'But we always kiss in the Middle East.' She paused and leaned forward conspiratorially. 'Usually just before we slit your throat...'

Leyla smiled and took in the young woman before her. Tala wore a soft shirt, open at the throat to reveal a thin, plain gold chain. Her nails were short and unpolished, her shoes immaculate, but flat and practical. Her hair was curly and untamed, and it lent her an air of slight madness, as though the thoughts in her head were springing directly out through her scalp. Leyla became aware that her face was advertising her surprise because Tala was watching her, amused.

'You're not what I expected.' Leyla spoke the most coherent sentence floating in her head and then closed her eyes slightly against her own forthrightness.

'That's because Ali paints me as a rich, spoilt princess,' Tala replied dryly.

'Isn't it true?' he asked her with gentle sarcasm.

'I'm not a princess,' she replied with a smile.

'Just rich and spoilt,' her father noted, filling in the gap with the punchline that Tala had deliberately left open for him.

She smiled and sat on the floor, waving away offers of a seat. Her gaze moved back to Leyla.

'And are you what my mother expected? I heard her giving you the third degree, even from the hallway.'

Reema cleared her throat in preparation for her own defence, which evidently her daughter was going to make necessary tonight. Even in front of guests, she had a habit of ignoring social niceties that was unbecoming and occasionally embarrassing.

'I'm not sure,' Leyla said, with a lack of wit that she immediately regretted.

'Mama.' Her mother addressed Tala in the Arabic style, by using her own title. 'I was having a polite conversation. She is a lovely girl.' Reema's eyes again passed over Leyla as she made this pronouncement, taking in the well-proportioned features, the glossy dark hair (which could be styled a little more) and the figure which was acceptable, although the girl clearly lacked the awareness of how to enhance her natural assets. She looked to be decent enough, perhaps lacking a little polish, but there was still the matter of her father's work that had to be flushed out.

'How many people work in your family's business?' Reema asked, by way of subtly gauging the size of the concern.

'About one in three,' Leyla quipped. It was a habit of hers, when she was self-conscious, to fall back on small jokes but she was immediately sorry for it. Reema regarded her blankly, and only the fact that she began the ritual of preparing another cigarette prevented Leyla from withering entirely under the older woman's gaze.

Tala, however, laughed.

'There are ten of us here,' Leyla replied quickly. 'And about ten in Africa – we have a couple of offices there.'

This pleased Reema immensely. 'A worldwide operation,' she said. An overblown and inaccurate vision of her father's business as a multi-national conglomerate passed briefly through Leyla's mind as she smiled politely at Reema.

'Mama,' Tala said. 'Ease up on the questions. She's marrying Ali, not me.'

Everyone laughed, but beneath the stretched tension of Reema's powdered face, her cheeks burned. It was an easy, flippant comment, but Tala's referral to marriage, to herself in relation to this girl; the throwaway suggestion of union between two women, set Reema's teeth on edge. She reached for the flaming palm tree once more and waited for the first drag on her cigarette to relax her.

'I hear you're getting married,' offered Leyla. 'Congratulations. That's wonderful news.'

Reema sat back and listened and decided that she liked this girl Leyla after all.

'You're welcome to come to the wedding, if you like, it's in six weeks,' offered Tala. 'Have you been to Jordan?'

Leyla had been nowhere in the Middle East. It spoke to her of starry nights and sand dunes (both images gleaned from 1970's Turkish Delight advertisements). It suggested liquid, smoky eyes glimpsed over a hijab, cardamom-infused coffee and romantic souks. She tried to communicate this to Tala with the necessary tone of irony, aware that Reema was regarding her strangely.

'The souk in Amman is a dump,' Tala informed her. 'But I can have someone take you there if you like.'

'That's kind of you,' Leyla replied. She was secretly shocked by the presumption that the sudden wedding invitation would be accepted. 'But I'm afraid I won't be able to come. I have to work.'

'Do you like it?'

'What?'

'Your work?'

Leyla hesitated. 'Mostly. It's finance and numbers, mainly.'

'But it's not your passion?'

She did not know how to answer such a question. It was the first time she had ever been asked it. She looked at Tala's eyes, softly brown, intent, alive.

'No,' she replied. 'Not my passion.'

Apparently unconscious of the impression she was making, Tala reached for the small tray of syrup-drenched pastries that accompanied the tea, offering them around before putting one into her mouth.

'Mama, we're having dinner in an hour,' Reema said reproachfully. 'And there is not a millimetre to spare in your wedding dress.'

'I'm not going to starve for another six weeks, Mama.' Tala ate another pastry and looked at Leyla. 'Join us for dinner?'

'I don't know, we...' she looked to Ali, but he was explaining supply chain economics to Tala's father. Quickly Leyla cast around for another question to ask.

'Will you get married in a mosque?' she asked, falling back on the wedding plans as an acceptable avenue for small talk. But she noticed Reema's eyebrows meet in a frown.

'A church,' Reema corrected. 'A church.'

'Not all Arabs are Muslims,' Tala said.

'I'm sorry, I shouldn't have assumed...' Leyla began, but Tala interrupted her.

'Are you a Muslim?'

Leyla wondered if Tala simply did not know how to ask questions about the weather. She sat up as she nodded. The ornate, carved chair in which she sat was becoming uncomfortable, but she felt an unusual pulse of energy moving through her limbs.

'Why?' Tala asked.

'Mama, what kind of a question is that?' Reema demanded. 'Because she was *born* a Muslim.'

'No, she wasn't,' said Tala.

'Weren't you?' Reema asked. Leyla felt her mouth opening uncertainly and then closing again, but Tala left no time for any reply.

'She was born female and a certain race,' Tala told her mother. 'And if she'd been adopted by a Jewish family, she'd have been Jewish.'

Reema sat back and exhaled a stream of cigarette smoke in relief. 'Thank God she wasn't adopted. What the Middle East doesn't need is more Jews!'

'Mama, please!' Tala closed her eyes, shook her head and sat back.

Out in the hallway Rani, the housekeeper who, as always, had travelled with Reema from Jordan, pushed out the swing door from the kitchen with her ample backside, for her hands were holding a silver tray carrying a crystal tumbler of water. She paused for a moment in the dim corridor, listening briefly as Reema expounded on politics and religion. She spat into the water, and then, with a slight flourish, dropped in a tablet of soluble painkiller that fizzed its way up the glass.

Leyla felt the room spin for a moment, but the moment passed. She forced herself to focus on the arrival of an Indian housekeeper, bearing a small gilt tray upon which a glass of effervescent liquid rested.

'Your headache medicine, Madam,' Rani said. Leyla watched the housekeeper intently, seeking respite from the aggression of the conversation, but found instead that the woman's eyes held what seemed like a malicious gleam as she watched Reema lift the glass to her lips.

'I don't have a headache,' Reema remembered suddenly. Rani's face dropped as she pushed the tray nearer.

'But it is seven o'clock, Madam. Your usual headache time.'

Despite the logic of this reply, Reema dismissed her with a flick of the hand, then rose and excused herself. She had no more than three quarters of an hour to re-apply her make up and get dressed for dinner. Even from the hallway, she could hear Tala's hectoring tone. The girl was lucky anyone would marry her, she thought to herself, let alone a gem like Hani.

'You didn't answer my question,' Tala said.

'I'm not Jewish,' Leyla answered with a slight smile.

Tala laughed. 'Why not?'

'Why aren't you?'

'I don't subscribe to any religion,' Tala explained.

'So you live without any faith?' asked Leyla, feeling more controlled now, more like her father. She waited for a response, but for a few moments Tala only met her gaze intently.

'I didn't say that,' she said gently.

Disarmed and disconcerted, Leyla looked away. 'Why should my beliefs offend you?'

'They don't,' Tala smiled. 'I just want to know why they don't offend you.'

Leyla suddenly longed for just a small touch of her father's sales techniques. He would never have let the conversation get this far out of hand. He would already have converted to Islam the woman with the expressive hair, sitting on the floor.

'Okay,' Leyla said, desperately. 'I've been brought up to follow this religion, this path. Is that so bad?' Leyla detected an edge of whining defensiveness in her own ears that was not attractive.

'Yes' Tala said. 'Why aren't you Jewish? Just by choosing one of these paths, you're implying there's something better about the one chosen, aren't you?'

'Maybe not better, just preferred,' Leyla replied.

'But did you prefer Islam? Or do you prefer it because it's what you were brought up with? How would your parents feel if you 'preferred' Judaism?'

'It's more than a preference,' Leyla said, desperately. 'It's faith.'

'I see,' Tala said, smiling. 'Faith. So no questioning allowed.'

'You just questioned me.'

'And you didn't proclaim a fatwa on my head,' she laughed. 'Thank you!'

The cold wind of the London night caught Leyla with violence on the side of her head as they left. Ali reached for her hand, but she could not bring herself to take hold of something which brought so little comfort, so little emotion of any kind. She felt raw, as though the scars had been picked from old, dried wounds, and the exposed cuts were now being dipped into salt water. She glanced up, towards the old lamps of the park, to the gracious brick buildings whose warm interiors spoke of comfortable, pleasurable lives. But these gave her not an ounce of consolation, no salve to spread over the mental beating she had just received.

They got into the car.

'Did you like them?' he asked.

'Oh, yes,' she replied and she was speaking the truth, at least partly. Some corner of her battered mind was grateful for the exchange that had just happened, was inspired by the simple, yet undeniably clear possibilities that this unknown girl had casually placed before her, as though offering a tray of sweetmeats. But the rest of her was relieved to sink into the leather seats of Ali's car and to shut the door and enclose herself in the small, warm space with only him beside her.

Chapter Three

T HEY HAD DINNER, just the three of them, at a nearby Italian restaurant. Omar had known the place for years from his constant visits to London, and liked it because the service was efficient and he was not made to wait half an hour between courses. Reema liked it because the lighting was sensitive to a woman's complexion and the clams in the spaghetti vongole were (correctly) removed from their shells, thereby saving her the irritating task of picking at stubbornly attached bits of seafood in the semi-darkness. Tala, on the other hand, had decided inwardly that she would never visit the restaurant again – it was gloomy inside, and the suspicions raised by the overly rapid service of the food were confirmed when she tasted it. Nothing was freshly cooked. Her father ate too quickly to fully taste anything, and her mother's taste buds must have been annihilated by years of heavy smoking. Her disappointment at the food was not relieved by the company of her parents. On the contrary, dinner conversation consisted primarily of listening to Reema hold forth about weddings, family gossip or, her new topic, Tala's attempt to set up her own business. Reema's insistent assessment of the requirements of her daughter's company was made from data she had gleaned perhaps twenty-five years ago, and was therefore lacking in any relevance whatsoever, but she enjoyed applying herself to management solutions all the same. Omar half-listened, while simultaneously counting the number of people in the restaurant, and checking the number of minutes between courses (he generally allowed ten minutes longer for the main course). This left Tala with the burden of listening and responding, if required, to her mother's soliloquys.

'If you're going to start making your own products, you should manufacture in India or Africa,' Reema was saying. 'Choose a poor country.'

Tala looked desperately for her father, but he had chosen that moment to go to the bathroom.

'Why?' she asked, willing herself to remain calm.

'Mama, its obvious,' Reema sighed, exasperated with her daughter's lack of acumen. 'They need the work. They're strong people, used to hard work. You can run factories twenty four hours a day and you can pay them virtually nothing. Isn't South America in big trouble now?' she asked rhetorically. 'You should try there. Then you could use your Spanish too.'

A spreading blotch of red appeared in Tala's mind – it was there when she closed her eyes momentarily. She could see it, could feel it, bleeding out at the edges, covering her whole internal frame of vision, until she was certain that when she opened her eyes, she would scream at her mother.

She opened her eyes. She reached for her water glass and took a sip, and she replaced it and she did not scream. Reema, incredibly, was still talking.

'Ali was telling us his grandfather had factories in India. All over the country. How do you think they became so well off?'

'They had factories in India, because they sold to the Indian market,' Tala said slowly. 'And they chose factories there because they lived and worked there, not so they could exploit poor people and make even bigger profits by overworking and underpaying them!'

Tala paused, aware that she was shouting, albeit in an undertone that had been adapted specifically for restaurant use. While she was taking a breath – and it was only one, quick breath – her mother managed to slip past and take over the conversation. It was as though she had heard nothing Tala had said.

'You can buy a factory in India for nothing,' her mother informed her. 'You can buy it, you can adapt it, and you'll never run out of cheap labour. Here they have rights; they can only work so many hours, and they have tea breaks, and lunch breaks, and minimum wages. There's no way for a business to make an honest profit. They have unions,' she added with distaste.

'For a reason,' Tala told her. 'To prevent exploitation. Would you like to work all day with no lunch? Or no minimum wage?'

And this, in a nutshell, was her daughter's problem, Reema thought. She asked questions that had no relevance to herself. Tala's lot in life was to own the companies that employed these people, and therefore her duty was to maximise the profits they made. If she was born on the other side, *then* let her lead a workers' mutiny. This last idea reminded her of another argument.

'Don't you remember how the trade unions brought this country to a standstill with all their strikes?'

'That was years ago,' Tala said irritably. 'The whole economic structure of this country is different now. It won't happen again.'

'They said that after the First World War, and look what happened twenty years later. Another war. Complacency,' Reema replied sagely.

Tala looked at her mother. She marvelled that, once again, she had been drawn down the path of what seemed like a standard (if ill-informed) discussion, only to find that she was trapped in a sticky morass of meaningless comparisons. She knew if she attempted to answer the war analogy she would only run up against an even more bizarre and unrelated argument.

'The bathrooms are very clean,' Omar said, sitting down. 'There are about twenty hand towels in each one.'

'Good,' Tala said, as though this was the news she had been waiting for the entire evening. 'I'll go.'

She took her time in the bathroom, splashing water onto her face, which was, to Reema's chagrin, free of make up. She blotted the cool drops from her forehead and cheeks slowly, gently, with one of the many hand towels, and her mind went back to the conversation with Leyla a couple of hours earlier. She had been harsh, she realised, and didn't know why. What was it about Ali's girlfriend that had inspired her to needle her in that way? Tala smiled briefly at the memory of Leyla's surprised face and then sighed, recalling her troubled eyes. She lingered at the basin for a few moments more, moments of quiet. Her parents would be gone the next day, Tala reminded herself, back to Amman, and she would remain here to work, alone, until she returned for the wedding.

To her relief, the bill had been paid when she returned, despite Reema's protests that she was still eating her tiramisu. The street and the fresh cold air of the night were a release after the compressed tension of the last hour and a half, but Tala found herself turning alone in the direction of their house.

'I want a few minutes in the casino, Omar,' Reema said. 'I feel lucky.' This statement was absolutely true. After the unpleasant moment Reema had suffered earlier that evening when Tala had made that comment about Leyla and marriage, things had slowly picked up. First, her daughter had proceeded to rattle the girl with her bizarre views on religion, no doubt offending her terribly in the end. Then Hani had called from Amman and after Reema had spent twenty minutes with him, ensuring that he was following up on all the necessary wedding preparations back home (he was), he and Tala had spent half an hour talking and laughing. Now, she felt, her daughter was considering the advice she had given on the factory. These were all good, reassuring signs.

On the quiet, lit street, Tala sighed. 'I'll meet you at home,' she said.

'Wait five minutes,' her father said. 'You and I can have a coffee while your mother loses some money.'

Reema paid no attention to this cynicism. The soft lights of the casino entrance, the handsome, tail-coated, top-hatted doorman who greeted her by name, the sleek cars that pulled up to the kerb, the unseen hands that whisked away her wrap, the chandeliers that lit the grand staircase leading up to the gaming rooms – all of these sent a quiver of excitement through her. Now she felt alive, now she felt all the distilled emotion of life pulsing in her veins. She sat down carefully on a velvet-swathed high chair and watched a few rounds of blackjack without playing. She waited, impatient but disciplined through years of experience, and then, with the first hand that went against the dealer, she laid her money on the table and took into her palm the short stack of chips that she received in return.

Tala looked at her mother, noted the widened, excited eyes that had watched her so narrowly throughout dinner, and she turned away, in time for Omar to steer her into a lounge, designed to evoke an English country library. Tala's irritation with her mother was being replaced with something deeper and more disturbing, a sense of dissatisfaction with herself; and below that lay a whole stratum of sorrow. In her disaffected state, she noticed at once that the 'library' was filled with whole shelves, whole walls, of fake books. The only reading material was a copy of a society magazine that had been laid on one of the coffee tables. Omar moved towards two deep leather chairs before a roaring gas fireplace and they sat down and Tala ordered herbal tea.

'No coffee?' Omar asked her.

She shook her head. 'I want to sleep tonight. I haven't been sleeping well.'

He considered asking her why this was the case, but hesitated in case he should uncover a can of emotional worms that he would have no idea how to deal with.

'I guess it's the wedding and everything,' she offered, knowing that if she wanted to attempt to speak to him, she would have to make the approach herself.

'You shouldn't worry,' he replied. 'Your mother and Lamia have everything under control.'

That was true, insofar as cutlery, dresses, jewellery and invitations went. Her sister Lamia's wedding two years before had been tastefully showy, and people in Amman still talked about it. Lamia and Reema, therefore, were judged to have impeccable credentials when it came to organising such events.

'Hani's a good man,' Omar offered, because he had been given to understand that the weighing up of the prospective groom was his territory. 'Like Kareem.'

She could not argue with that either. Hani was very good, and had survived every rigorous test she had internally and silently put him through. Like her father, she had unconsciously begun the process by comparing him to Lamia's husband, Kareem. But the more she observed the latter, the more she became aware that Kareem shone mostly by comparison to other Arab men, rather than in his own right. Tala had therefore quickly discarded this method of evaluation for Hani, and had refused to be grateful that he had no issue with having a wife who worked for a living, for example. But even as she raised the bar, Hani contrived, unconsciously, to reach it. He really was extremely intelligent, emotionally aware, sensitive to her moods. He was also hard-working and handsome. In the six months that they had been together, they had discussed everything, from sex to politics to religion, and the more outrageous of her views succeeded not in turning him away, but in making him think, and then argue back coherently, or adapt his own ideas accordingly. In short, she had been unable to find one single reason why she should not marry him.

'Baba,' Tala said. She swallowed, but knowing that there would rarely be a better time, determined to ask her father the question that was in her mind. 'How did you know you wanted to marry Mama?'

Her father shifted uncomfortably. This was not the kind of thing he had ever expected or hoped to discuss with his daughters. But he felt trapped by Tala's earnest gaze. He fought the urge to panic blindly, like a fly in a bottle, and simply shrugged.

'I saw her once,' he said. 'And I knew she was the one for me.'

The ostensible romanticism of this reply became less obvious when Tala considered that she could indeed understand that this might have been the case – it was only when her mother began talking at length that most people realised her limitations.

'But after you got to know her,' Tala pressed. 'Did it just stay with you, that feeling?' Omar looked bewildered, and she felt that she was losing him. She tried again, desperately.

'Did you just become more sure she was right for you? Didn't you ever doubt it?'

Omar hailed the waiter and asked for the bill. When he had recovered himself somewhat, by counting out coins and notes and then re-aligning them before folding them back neatly into his money clip, he spoke.

'Tala,' he said at last. 'Don't think about everything so much.'

And then Reema called to them from the edge of the room. Quickly, Omar swallowed the last of his tea and stood up to greet his wife, who stood stiffly, avoiding their gaze. Purely from this posture, Tala could tell that the money was lost, and her father read the situation also. He smiled.

'What do you have to smile about?' Reema snapped.

'I had a lovely cup of tea with Tala,' he said. 'And it only cost me five hundred pounds. Plus the tip for the limousine,' he grinned, reaching into his pocket.

Reema turned on her heel and walked back through the hallway, pausing to collect her fur wrap from the attendant, and motioning to her husband to give the girl a tip as she passed. Omar did so, and helped Tala on with her coat. Outside, Reema swept into a waiting Rolls Royce, provided with the compliments of the casino management to save them the three hundred yard walk back to their home. Tala watched her mother's angry profile as she sat in the back of the car and stared straight ahead, and knew that she would be frustrated that the cards had cheated her. She took all gambling losses personally, could not bring herself to understand it as a game of chance in which the odds were forever stacked a little against her.

'If she saw it that way, she wouldn't do it,' her father had told Tala once. 'She thinks she's controlling it.'

Reema's argument was that she was controlling it, that there were rules, and if, for example, you took a card against a high number then you ruined the table for everyone else. Rules were of paramount concern to Reema, particularly when flouting the accepted conventions could throw off the people around you, and she had, in moments of deep introspection, considered that the principles she applied to blackjack held true for life itself. One strove to be noticed within the game of life, to be successful by rising above the other players who were all following the same route as yourself. And one rose in a number of ways – by achieving greater financial wealth than the others, or by marrying better, and by having good-looking children who got excellent degrees and then married well themselves. These were the basic blocks upon which all other desires were finely balanced. Once these foundations were in place, one could finesse one's success with smaller, but equally impressive achievements (keeping a youthful appearance, training an excellent cook for entertaining, learning bridge to tournament level). One did not step outside the game and try to begin a separate game. Nobody would play with you if you did; or worse – how could you tell if you were doing everything correctly? The rules were tried and tested and had worked well for centuries, possibly millennia, though her knowledge of history and anthropology did not extend far enough for her to affirm the millennia argument with conviction. In any case, it seemed to her that this idea that you could make your own rules and then delight in spitting in the face of society, was the fatal flaw in western education today. Original thought, in Reema's view, had very little to recommend it. Lamia had seen through this pitfall correctly, and Tala also, at last. But she worried about Zina, over in New York, now talking about taking a Phd in International Relations. She would speak to Omar about it again tomorrow. She did not want a daughter who was a doctor, unless she could at least prescribe pills.

Chapter 4

LEYLA WAS LOST, and happily so. In the quiet of her room, which the occasional birdsong from the garden made tangible, she sat at her desk, entangled in her writing, entwined with another life, with people she had never met but whom she had created. It made the bellowing of her name up the stairs by her mother all the more of a shock.

'Leyla!' Maya called, at a pitch designed to be noticed. 'He'll be here soon!'

Concentrate, Leyla, told herself. Hold on to the moment. For a few seconds more, she typed desperately, but the enchantment had been shattered. With a sigh, Leyla slid back her chair and went downstairs. She moved quietly, lightly on her feet, as though entering the kitchen unobtrusively might help ease her into real life. But Maya was waiting at the door, waving a wooden spoon.

'I don't understand why Ali can't eat with us first!'

Leyla exchanged a glance with her sister Yasmin, who kept one eyebrow raised sardonically, even while chopping lettuce.

'He's booked a tennis court, Mum. With two other friends of his.'

'At one o'clock? That's lunchtime.'

'Only in the Suburban time zone, Mum,' explained Yasmin helpfully. 'I think London is two hours ahead of us.'

Maya shook her head irritably. More than twenty years of her life she had given to raising these girls and all she got in return was attitude.

'What kind of salad are you making anyway?' she asked her younger child accusingly, in the absence of any other immediate issue to pounce on.

'A Greek salad,' Yasmin replied placidly. She began stoning olives.

'And Indian salad is not good enough, apparently.'

Yasmin laughed. 'What is an Indian salad? Three week old lettuce and chillis?'

Leyla laughed but Maya was incensed. 'You two are so worried about other cultures. London! Greece! What about your own heritage? Did you ever think about that? India has one of the richest cultures in the world!'

'I'm glad you said that because I'm thinking of spending six months out there,' Yasmin said, flicking olive stones into the sink where they landed with a satisfying ring. She paused before delivering the final blow. 'Backpacking.'

It was clear to Maya, in this moment, that her daughters were intent on sending her to an early grave. She read the newspapers, she watched the news, and she knew that backpacking could mean only three things – hitch-hiking, rape and murder, in that order. The issue of hygiene was also foremost in her mind, but she supposed that if you were headed for a bloody death, then clean underwear was perhaps the least of your problems. She could feel another hair turning white as she thought about it, a hair on the front of her head where it would be most visible. She would ignore Yasmin for now, and later on she would talk to Sam and make sure he forbade any backpacking. And in India, of all places.

The soothing chime of the doorbell interrupted Maya's thoughts and she greeted Ali effusively, for she liked him. Even in tennis gear, he looked neatly turned out and handsome. She watched as he greeted Yasmin.

'Something smells good in here,' he smiled.

'Feta cheese. My Greek salad,' she noted with a pointed glance at Maya.

'I didn't know you could cook,' said Ali, teasing. Maya smiled, but looked around for Leyla. The girl was always hanging back when she should be pushing herself forward.

'Of course she can cook,' Maya assured him. 'And so can Leyla.' Maya drew her eldest daughter into the circle. 'She makes the best cakes, and never puts on weight!'

'We should be going,' interrupted Leyla. 'Come on.' Guiding Ali back to the front door, she ignored Maya's final exhortation that they should stay for lunch instead of playing tennis, and with a satisfying click, she closed the front door behind them before exchanging a look with the smiling Ali.

When Leyla discovered they would be playing with Tala, as well as Jeff, another friend of Ali's, a breath of anticipation shivered over her, even as her memory of their first meeting irritated her. For some reason, and without consulting her, Ali had already decided that the men and the women should each play singles. Tala looked professional in her immaculate white dress, and for the first time since buying them, Leyla eyed her own mismatched shorts and shirt with a detached and critical eye. But she knew she was good at tennis, naturally athletic and she warmed up with quiet confidence.

Her first attempt at serving slapped limply into the net. Leyla rolled her shoulders a little and geared up again, watching as Tala took an exaggerated step forward into the court. This step, the implication that she needed to be nearer to return the slow service Leyla would surely provide, annoyed Leyla intensely. She threw the ball up, watched it descend and sprang up to meet it with the grace of a panther pouncing on its prey. With a satisfyingly loud thwack, her racket smacked it, but it caught the edge of the net and fell back onto her own side. Leyla cursed under her breath. Tala smiled.

'They have a really good coach here. If you want a lesson.'

Now Leyla smiled grimly and turned away, wondering if there was any end to this woman's arrogance. She returned to her base line, and took a breath, for she understood now that it was no longer tennis, but war. Eyes narrowed on both sides. Sensing an impending storm, Tala stepped backwards this time, cradling her racket, primed for action. The service was hard and low to the ground, but Tala reached it and got the ball back into play, starting a pounding rally.

Forty minutes later, Ali and his opponent stopped to watch. The ball spun back and forth like a thing possessed, as feet pounded and slid, and rackets flailed. Leyla was only dimly aware that her hair was all over the place and her shirt was stuck to her ribs as she reached for a final serve that would give her the match. In a puff of clay, it shot past Tala, untouched.

'You did it,' Tala said, coming to the net. Her handshake was warm and her arm came up to hug Leyla's shoulders in congratulations.

'You're really good,' Tala said.

'You're not so bad yourself,' Leyla panted.

'Come on, let's get changed.'

Tala busied herself with looking for her shower things for a few minutes.

'How did you get that last game?' she asked. 'I thought I had it.'

'I prayed for divine intervention,' Leyla returned. The reply had a sardonic edge. Tala looked up at her, eyes serious.

'Look. I didn't say there wasn't a God. It's just religion that bothers me. I'm sorry if I offended you the other day,' she said.

Leyla looked away from her. 'No, actually, you made me think.'

'About what?'

'About why we follow certain paths. Is it just expectation? Or conditioning?'

Abruptly, as if she had revealed too much, Leyla broke off and turned away, catching her hand on a locker as she did so. Tala heard the buried gasp of pain and went to her, taking her hand, which only seemed to fluster Leyla more.

'It's fine, I'm just clumsy.'

Tala held onto the bruised fingers and waited till Leyla met her look.

'You know, you should really relax more. Just be at ease with yourself.'

Tala felt Leyla try to hold her gaze easily, try to relax her shoulders and her stance, but she only succeeded in looking more endearingly awkward. She let go of Leyla's hand, gently, and picked up her things.

'What are you doing tomorrow?'

'I'm supposed to have lunch with my family. Sunday and all that.'

Tala nodded and moved towards the showers, from where they could hear the languid echo of slow, full drips of water.

'Why?' called Leyla, hesitantly, after her. Tala turned.

'Nothing. I was just going to ask you if you wanted to have lunch. Maybe take a walk in the park.' She hesitated. 'I'd like to know you better.'

'You just want someone to argue with,' Leyla smiled.

'What if I promise to behave myself? Will you consider it?' Tala asked, and this time, she had to look away from something in Leyla's eyes as she nodded her assent.

In order to meet Tala for lunch on Sunday, Leyla had to contrive a way to extricate herself from a lunch party to be attended by numerous members of her extended family. This caused considerable consternation to her mother and father, who wanted to know what kind of last minute engagement could be so important that it meant missing lunch with her ailing grandmother and three cousins from Canada. Leyla knew that having lunch with a girl she barely knew but really liked, would not pass muster as a good enough reason, and so, under pressure, had rashly invented a date with Ali. As soon as she had uttered the excuse, she felt the acid taste of regret in her mouth, regret that she had resorted to lying, that she had lacked the strength to deal with her parents openly; but it was too late. The simple mention of his name smoothed the dismay on her mother's face, only to pave the way for a new hurdle.

'Bring him home for lunch,' Maya said. 'Then he can meet everybody.'

The idea of exposing Ali to the voracious gaze of her cousins horrified her. They were all racing each other towards marriage as if it were some sort of Olympic sport for which they had been in training since puberty. Equally disquieting was the idea of her grandmother's questions, which would doubtless be focused around the number of children they might be planning to have, and whether red saris or white were best for modern weddings. So appalled was she by this vision that it took her a moment to remember that she had just lied about Ali, and that he would be safely watching the rugby in his own flat all afternoon.

'I can't bring him here. He has an important business lunch,' she added, desperately.

'On a Sunday?' her father asked. He was always sharper than her mother, but luckily Maya's ecstatic response drowned out the question.

'And he wants you to be there? That's a good sign!' Maya opened the oven, letting out a blast of eyebrow-singeing heat that made her start cursing her husband for the brand new kitchen appliances he had forced on her.

'They're too hot! Too efficient!' she complained. 'Everything cooks in half the time, I don't know where I am any more.'

'If everything's cooking so quickly, you should be reading the newspapers with me,' Sam replied, but she gave him only her silent, sulking back and so he went through to the living room. Leyla remained in the kitchen, her immediate distress at her mother's mood and her own lies preventing her from taking any useful action. She glanced around. The salad was half prepared, the rice was waiting to be rinsed, and the table had still to be laid. She picked up the dull-edged knife (her mother had never used the finely honed set of Japanese knives that her Yasmin had given her the year before) and tried to slice tomatoes. It was not easy, because you had to know, from years of familiarity, exactly which tiny section of the old blade was still sharp, in order to press it down correctly and achieve a clean cut. In her anxiety, Leyla succeeded only in flattening the top of the overripe tomato and squashing out a pile of wet seeds onto the chopping board.

'What are you doing?' Maya asked before answering her own question. 'Ruining good tomatoes.'

'These tomatoes haven't been good since last week,' Leyla told her. 'They're overripe.'

'They're full of flavour,' corrected her mother. 'Nobody likes a sour, hard tomato.'

Leyla knew from experience that such a discussion could continue indefinitely if she allowed it to. Incongruously, an image flashed into her mind of a real discussion, of an important debate. Perhaps she could ask Maya how exactly she knew that she followed the correct religion. If she had been born Catholic, would she not be predisposed and educated to believe that Catholicism was the best way?

'What is it?' Maya asked. 'Why are you standing there like that?'

'I was just thinking.'

'Think about the guests,' her mother replied. 'And set the table.'

Leyla did so, quickly, and then retreated silently into the living room, where her father was reading the business section of the newspaper while listening to a political debate on television.

'Can you be back early?' he asked her. 'It would be nice if you could see your grandmother for a few minutes.'

'I'll try,' she said.

'And bring Ali with you, if you can.'

'I'll see if I can.'

She shifted slightly, and he looked at her over the top of his newspaper, and his eyes were clear and knowing, she thought. She felt exposed, and swallowed, leaning in to hear whatever it was that he might want to tell her.

'There's an article here you should read,' he said. 'About the best balance of assets in a pension fund.' He folded the paper and passed it into her hands. 'Let me know what you think.'

The day was overcast but the subtle light seemed to Leyla to soften the edges of the river and the trees as she walked with Tala through the park after lunch. They had spoken a lot over their meal, exchanged information and ideas, had gotten to know each other's family backgrounds and work and other tangible facts. Now, though, in the park, they walked for a few moments silently but together. There was space here, an open sky, a breath of wind to cast off the outer web of their conversation and to leave them time to pause. Pretending to look out at the river, Leyla glanced sideways at Tala. Her soft curls hung over her collar and in the dim, cool light, the rich brown of her hair seemed to glint with a light of its own.

'You know, you told me what you do, but not why you do it.' Tala said.

'What do you mean?'

Tala looked at her. 'You work for your father. The way I used to work for mine. But it's not what I really wanted to do.'

'And your new business is?'

Tala shrugged. 'It might be. I like the idea behind it. To create a market here using Palestinian suppliers of soaps and candles, things like that. It means working on product design and quality, and then selling them into shops. I enjoy the work. And it could make a difference to the quality of life of the people making them. And maybe give me a bit more independence.' Tala looked away, as if the last comment had touched too much on the personal.

'I hope you succeed. I'm sure you will.'

Tala smiled. 'And you? Do you like working with your father?'

Leyla gave a slight laugh. 'I don't mind it. He always wanted me to work with him. And there was nothing else I ever wanted to do except...' She broke off, surprised with herself for having come so close to revelation. She quickened her pace slightly, but it was too late. Tala had caught the moment and was now catching hold of her arm.

'Except what?'

Leyla stopped walking and laughed a little, nervously.

'Writing,' she answered. 'Fiction'. It was a tense moment for her, the cracking open of the door to a secret life that few people knew existed. 'I've had a few short stories published. And now I'm working on a novel.'

'Can I read your work?'

'I don't know.'

Tala laughed. 'Why? You don't trust me yet?'

'It's not that.'

'Okay. If you let me read something, you can ask me anything you like.'

Leyla looked at her. 'Anything?'

'Yes.'

'How did you manage to be engaged four times?' she asked quickly, then laughed at Tala's rolled eyes. 'I mean, you seem so decisive.'

'Well, I'm not proud of it,' said Tala. 'The first one – well, I was very young, and had no idea what I was getting into. The second one produced tonnes of dates. Which is great, and I love dates, but I didn't love him. The third one ticked all the boxes – good family, Christian Arab, intelligent, handsome. But it just didn't click.' She looked to Leyla for understanding and received it in the glance back.

'What about you and Ali?' Tala asked. 'How's that going?' They had slowed to a halt now, under the protective, enclosing branches of an oak tree. Beyond them, the river flowed with a soft sigh. Tala watched Leyla as she hesitated. Her eyes were clear, her skin almost translucent in the pale light.

'He's nice. I like him a lot.'

Tala nodded. 'But does it click?'

'Not the way I imagine it should.'

Tala felt a sudden impulse to brush away a long strand of dark hair that had fallen across Leyla's face. But she kept her hands in her jacket pocket and watched as Leyla pushed it away herself.

'Maybe we expect too much,' Tala said, suddenly. She felt Leyla watching her, trying to catch hold of her eyes to read what lay in them, but Tala remained intent on looking at the sky where thunder now lay crouched and grumbling. The smell of the coming storm hung in the air, metallic, strange.

'Come, we should go,' Tala said. 'It's going to rain.'

Chapter 5

LEYLA SPENT THE DRIVE home from the park veering between elation and uncertainty and it was the elation that was causing the uncertainty. She had just had lunch and a walk in the park with a friend. She should have been thinking of something else entirely by now, or at best reliving a couple of moments, not thinking over every nuance of every word and look that she had exchanged with Tala. In fact, she should be thinking of someone else entirely. Ideally Ali, or someone like him. But it was not Ali who was captivating her and this fact was one she had only just acknowledged openly to herself as she turned into her driveway and got out of the car. She had not had time to begin to consider the implications of the fact that she found the cadences of Tala's accent beautiful. Or that she was constantly surprised by the incisive articulation of the thoughts behind those brown eyes. That every time they exchanged a glance of communication her stomach fluttered. Or that, without even meaning to, she had already begun to lie to her parents in order to see Tala. There was a familiar pattern here, this much Leyla was forced to admit. She had been the victim of a series of silent yearnings throughout her late teens and early twenties. Some of these had lasted a few days; the majority had lasted a period of months and a couple for even longer. What they all had in common was that the attraction was usually hidden, forever unspoken, and always unre-quited. Although she had tried to think up other reasons why this had always been the case (for example, that the object of her desire was often married), she had now and then admitted the truth to herself, usually in the depths of the long Surrey night, under cover of the forgiving darkness – and the truth was that every one of these attractions had been to other women.

The fact that most of these affairs remained locked away in her own mind, occasionally struck her as a little feeble, but she found it easier to keep it all inside her than to try and disseminate it to those around her. And grasping this particular reality would be like taking hold of a cobra by its grinning face. The consequences would be so far reaching; the debris after the explosion would splinter into every part of her life and hurt everyone she knew. Not that this potential meltdown was a reason to lie to herself, she knew, but up until now, it had happened that all the women she had liked in that way were unavailable, uninterested or entirely unconscious of the situation and this had largely removed from Leyla's shoulders the burden of deciding what to do in the event of an actual relationship. She had no idea how one met women that might be open to such a union without responding to internet postings, or sifting all one's acquain-tances according to various unreliable stereotypes. And if she did that, it seemed too ridiculous that Ann Framer, her friend in the last year of school, should potentially be classified in the wrong box be-cause she was good at tennis and liked cats. What she wanted, what she one day hoped for, was a simple, mutual attraction. A moment of understanding. An overwhelming impulse that revealed the hid-den passion to be right and true.

'You want the good news or the bad news?'

Leyla jumped, then sighed, relieved to be greeted by her sister, despite the fact that Yasmin seemed highly irritated.

'What's the bad news?'

'Ali – who you were supposedly out with today – called to ask if you wanted to go over and watch the rugby.'

Leyla closed her eyes. 'Oh, no. Tell me you answered the phone?'

'Well, see,' said Yasmin. 'That's the good news. Dad did. AND – he didn't tell Mum.'

Leyla tried to slip past and into her room, consumed by a head spinning mélange of fading excitement from her day with Tala and guilt at upsetting her father. But Yasmin blocked her way.

'Not so fast. You owe me. Big time. Leaving me alone with the cousins from hell. And not even for Ali. Where were you anyway?'

Since returning from Nairobi, Yasmin had begun to suspect that her older sister was enjoying some sort of double life. Although that phrase might be an overstatement – what Yasmin had intuited was more of a hidden aspect, an interior world, as yet insubstantial and undefined. She took pleasure in the idea because for too long, Yasmin had been all alone in the vanguard of fights for liberty of action, thought and speech against her parents, while Leyla, it seemed, had been content to accept the terms of the small dictatorship without complaint, on the grounds that she had no compelling reason to revolt. Despite being two years younger, it was Yasmin who had been the first to decline the offer of a place in the family business; who had left home and lived on her own in Kenya; and it was Yasmin who had first had a boyfriend. This apparent lack of need, the lack of desire, which Yasmin found in her sister – for privacy, for wider experiences, for men, had confused and annoyed her intensely.

Since her return, however, and even more noticeably in the past couple of weeks, Leyla had seemed more real – more like a person in her own right. The regular rhythms of their lives in the vast, old, Surrey house had not changed, but that afternoon's amazing development, the uncovering of a lie from Leyla of all people, had sharpened Yasmin's sense that her sister was changing. As uplifted as she was by this idea (for Leyla's sake, as well as her own – and it would be so good to have someone to fight with her), she still did not want to let go of the fact that Leyla had knowingly abandoned her in hell for the entire afternoon. Yasmin led the way up to the third floor attic space which her father had converted into a larger room for her, complete with her own sitting area and small bathroom, while she was away. He had done this to 'incentivise' her to return (a crucial element in retaining key company employees, he explained, and he saw no reason why the principle could not extend to family members too), an attempt which Yasmin recognised as bribery, even as she accepted the offered space. They sat at opposite ends of a sagging blue sofa.

'You're having an affair with someone, aren't you?' was Yasmin's opening line. She grinned. 'And it's not Ali. Is he English? Even better, is he black? Mum will die.'

Leyla tried to sigh but could only smile. 'No, on all counts.'

Yasmin looked deeply disappointed. 'Are you sure?'

'I think I'd notice if I was having an affair. I just went to hang out with a new friend of mine. But you know you practically need a medical certificate to miss our family events.'

Yasmin's sigh attested to the truth of this statement. 'I need to get my own place,' she said. 'So do you.'

They considered this silently for a few moments. Neither of them had nearly enough money for a deposit on a flat. Nor would their parents sanction a move out of the family house without a marriage certificate.

'Why don't you just marry Ali? You'd be out of here at least.'

'You know why I won't just marry him,' Leyla said sharply. 'I don't love him, and he doesn't love me.'

'Then why are you going out with him?' Yasmin asked quietly.

There was no succinct reply to this question. The answer would always be unconvincing and was caught up in a complex tangle of issues, including the fact that Ali was fun to be around, that the relationship pleased her parents and gave her time to try and overcome her own natural leanings.

'Who's your new friend?' Yasmin asked. Her gaze was sharper now and her back was straighter. Although Yasmin moved through life at a pace that seemed guaranteed to allow no reflection, she was in fact acutely sensitive to the motivations of every one of her family members. And at this moment, Yasmin recalled that Leyla had been playing the new kd lang CD almost non stop recently.

'I met her through Ali,' Leyla said, and she damped down the smile that unconsciously came to her face.

Her, thought Yasmin. Strike one. She would have to tread carefully and change tack if she was to probe this further.

'Can I ask you something?'

'Sure,' Leyla replied.

'Have you done this often?' Yasmin asked casually. 'Lied to Mum and Dad?'

'Never,' said Leyla, crestfallen. 'I can't believe I did it.'

Strike two, thought Yasmin. She's already lying for this girl.

'Is she nice-looking?' Yasmin asked. Immediately, she realised this was far too obvious a strategy. Leyla immediately stiffened and laughed, and asked what kind of question that was. Though her obvious discomfort might in fact be a further clue. Never mind, Yasmin thought. She would leave it alone for now. There would be time to sniff out the details later. Maybe she would follow Leyla down to her room, pretend to look for a missing shirt or something. She was sure she'd seen a DVD of 'The L Word' lying around. That might be all the extra evidence she needed.

'Anyway,' Yasmin said, to break her sister's awkwardness. 'Congratulations.'

'For what?'

'Defying your parents today.'

Leyla gave a bitter half-laugh. 'I didn't defy them, I lied to them.'

'Well, it's a start,' Yasmin said, determined to find a modicum of hope in the situation. 'Now you just have to learn to do it with the truth.'

'But they make it so difficult, don't they?' Leyla said, savagely. 'I can't bear the way they make such dramas out of every little thing. Every little deviation from their plans.'

'Don't blame them,' Yasmin told her. 'You've let them ignore you as a person for too long. If there's one thing I've learned, it's always to make sure your drama is bigger than theirs. If they shout, shout louder. If they sulk, sulk harder.'

'I don't want to have to play those games,' replied Leyla, and she stood up.

'Sweetheart,' Yasmin said. 'Life is a game. And if you don't want to miss it, you better get playing.'

Leyla liked to think that it was this advice from her sibling that led her to be sitting alongside Tala the following evening in the warmth and darkness of a London theatre. On an impulse, Leyla had called to invite her new friend to see a play, and Tala had accepted with alacrity. The actors had been on stage for perhaps twenty minutes, and Leyla watched them moving about and talking, gradually re-alising that she had no idea what the plot was about, or who the characters were.

For all her senses, all her perceptions were trained on just one small part of her body, the side of her forearm, which lay on the armrest between herself and Tala. When the curtain had risen, she had sensed Tala's arm raise also, had felt it shift onto the narrow, velvet bridge between them, and she had almost pulled her own arm away, to give her more room. But the touch of Tala's shirt against her bare skin had thrilled her, and it felt wonderful to have that con-nection with the girl beside her and she had remained there, with as much nonchalance as she could muster. When the audience laughed at a line, she smiled also, though she had no idea of what had been said, and took the opportunity to cast a sideways glance at Tala. Tala turned to meet the look, then leaned to whisper in Leyla's ear.

'I forgot to ask – did you bring your stories?'

Leyla nodded and looked back at the stage, feeling her bag against her feet, the bag which contained two rolled up magazines which contained her short stories. She had been excited about giving them to Tala, had been just a little proud that Tala would see her name in print. But now she felt more than a strong misgiving that as soon as she read the stories, Tala would hate them. Every phrase in her writing that Leyla had ever been uncertain about began to haunt her. She wondered if the emotions they described were not trite and unreal. She coughed and tried to focus on the play.

'Don't worry.' Tala's voice was there again, unexpectedly, in her ear. 'I'll love them.'

At exactly the same time on the following evening, Leyla found herself in a fluorescent-lit supermarket aisle with her mother and sister, a setting that could not have been further removed from the softly-lit, enticing ambience of the previous night's theatre with Tala. But to Leyla, as she spoke on her mobile phone, the unvarying rows of neatly stacked produce seemed fresh and glowing. Even in the last twenty-four hours, she had missed Tala's voice, had longed to hear its particular inflections and intonations, had missed the sharpness and the softness that it could so easily and equally encompass.

'You haven't returned my calls,' Tala said.

'You left one message,' Leyla said, smiling. 'This morning. I was going to call you later.'

'I hope that's true.'

'It is.'

Leyla glanced up at her sister, casually, and Yasmin caught the look, conquered her instinct to eavesdrop and quickly went off to choose a brie.

In the ensuing pause Leyla felt the blood rise up to her cheeks. She could think of nothing to say, nothing that was acceptable and friendly, no phrase to move the conversation on, no question that would not open up her heart like the quiet slit of a scalpel.

'Why did you call?' Leyla asked.

'I wanted to thank you for last night,' she offered at last. 'But more than that, to thank you for giving me your stories to read. I loved them. You are very talented Leyla.'

Leyla felt herself blush and stammered out her thanks, which Tala interrupted.

'Would you like to come with me to Oxford at the weekend? My family are sponsoring a lecture series about Jordan. And we have a meeting at one of the colleges there to discuss starting it in Oxford.' Tala hesitated, before adding 'My sister Lamia will be there. She's flying in from Jordan.'

'Okay,' Leyla said.

'Really?'

Leyla laughed. 'Really.'

She looked up to find her mother watching her from the fish counter, and she moved casually away to continue the conversation.

Maya had heard Ali's phone call come in that Sunday but had been unable to get any sense out of her husband. She suspected, therefore, that something had been hidden from her, but by Monday evening, as she led her daughters through the supermarket, she decided against instigating a formal investigation. Maya looked over at Leyla, and a smile touched her face. Her daughter was skulking around the Tinned Fruit and Veg aisle, whispering into her mobile phone, blushing and giggling. Obviously, Ali was on the phone, managing the situation perfectly, for her daughter was finally behaving exactly as Maya had always hoped – like a young woman in love.

She turned away and back to the fish counter, where the whole fish she had selected had now been weighed and priced. The shock of the number that the woman in the soiled white apron had just spoken jolted Maya out of her thoughts of Leyla's wedding and focused her attention on the ice-packed counter before her. Maya wavered. She could easily afford the fish; that was not the issue. Whether it was value for money was the question. Thank God Yasmin was at the cheese counter and not there to pressure her. But there was a short line of people queuing behind her. Ranged along the display of clear-eyed dead fish, each one of them was watching her, politely but with quiet intimidation, waiting for her to accept the specimen that she had requested and move on. She calculated in her head – perhaps she should just buy six or eight fillets, but would the saving be worth the difference in prestige when she produced a beautiful dish of masala fish?

'I'll take it,' she said. She felt an immediate elation at having made a decision – the right decision – before doubts again assailed her. Perhaps the fish was too showy. After all, she was contributing food to a post-funeral gathering, for in their community it was traditional that no food was prepared in the house of the deceased. She would be taking this enormous, gleaming salmon to a house where a death had just occurred. A subdued house, a house of mourning, a house where simple food should be the order of the day. She now realised that she had just spent fifty pounds to purchase a fish she couldn't use. One that her family would now have to eat, when she could have fed them with four fillets at a cost of two pounds and ninety nine pence each. Dazed, Maya accepted the plastic-wrapped fish corpse and pushed her trolley over to where the toilet rolls were.

'You see,' Yasmin's voice chimed in behind her. 'If you ordered online, you wouldn't need to schlep loo rolls around. They could just deliver them.'

Maya ignored her and looked gratefully at the toilet rolls. These, at least, were on special offer. One pound off a pack of nine. So that if she bought around four hundred rolls of toilet paper, she could recoup the price of the fish. Why did they make trolleys so small? She felt like weeping. Every day, life was full of such uncertainties, such decisions, such disappointments. Without her faith in God and her conviction that there was an afterlife where there was peace, she could not have survived the daily pitfalls of existence. Without her faith that He had an ultimate plan for her in this life, that He had made her buy the fish for a reason, she would simply cave in and give up. Something within these last thoughts made her stop dead. She stopped piling toilet paper into the trolley and considered. He had made her buy the fish for a reason. And that reason was suddenly completely clear. The funeral was for a member of the Surti family. They were rich. Obscenely wealthy, in fact. Of course she should prepare the fish for them. The dead man had undoubtedly been used to such dishes, had probably demanded them daily from their cook (they had three, she had heard). It would be exactly right, extremely appreciated, and perfectly impressive. Maya smiled.

'Mum?' Leyla said, switching off her mobile as they queued at the checkout. 'I'm going to Oxford this weekend.'

'Oxford? Why Oxford? Oxford's where you go to get a degree, not to get away.'

Leyla said nothing, just looked mutely at Yasmin, who sighed and started unloading the trolley.

'It's only an hour away. Why do you have to go for a weekend?'

'So if it takes me three hours I can spend the night?' Leyla snapped.

'Who are you going with?' Maya asked Leyla. Now Yasmin cast a sly glance across at her sister who folded her arms crossly.

'Nobody. A friend. They have some work there.'

A knowing smile began to crease over Maya's face. 'Ooh. Ali!'

'No, not Ali. Does everything have to revolve around him?' Leyla's voice held pure irritation now.

'I don't understand,' Maya said plaintively.

'What is there to understand?' Yasmin interrupted. 'She has a friend, she's invited her to Oxford for a weekend. I don't see the problem.'

Neither could Maya, when the situation was laid out in this way, but she refused to be upset for no reason. If it took all day, she would find one. She turned to Yasmin who was staggering under the weight of the wrapped salmon.

'What do you have in here, Mum? Moby Dick?'

'Just be careful with that fish, young lady. It cost me an arm and a leg.'

'And it might eat everything else in the trolley,' commented Yasmin. Leyla smiled at the joke, but was disconcerted to find that under her surface smirk, Yasmin's eyes were watching her piercingly. She looked away and started to pack carrier bags with groceries, resolving to call Ali when she got home and alleviate her guilt.

Chapter 6

L AMIA ARRIVED IN OXFORD for the lecture meetings armed with her father's credit card and her mother's detailed instructions regarding Tala's trousseau. Though what she was expected to buy in Oxford, she wasn't sure. The place was pretty enough, but it was also all museums and culture. As far as she knew, there wasn't even a Gucci. Still, it was the first time since her marriage that Lamia had travelled without her husband, who had remained in Amman, working, since the dual purpose of her trip (charitable lectures, shopping for a wedding) were not events he could justify leaving his work for. She had enjoyed her solo flight tremendously and felt a certain guilty freedom in travelling alone. All of her journeys with Kareem were meticulously planned, and there was undoubtedly a positive side to this, since her husband's conscientiousness allowed her to slip into a kind of auto-pilot mode where she did not have to worry about anything like passports, timings or packing; but in the end she also found their trips emotionally draining. For Kareem had a tendency to be compulsive. His clothes, for example, had to be folded in a certain way and he would allow neither the staff nor Lamia herself to actually place them into the suitcase. He had a system for packing, as he had systems for almost everything, and the proper adherence to the packing system ensured that he could fit a maximum number of garments (plus one hardback book, business-related, and a washbag) into his suitcase, without causing anything to crease unnecessarily. This aspect of his personality had been one of his attractions for Lamia during the brief period when they had been dating. Within Lamia burned a hollow of insecurity, which Tala and Zina had together traced back to her unfulfilled need for their mother's attention (as the middle child she had been even more overlooked than the other two), compounded by the lack of a strong character of her own. Lamia herself was not convinced by such Americanised psycho-babble. All she knew was that Kareem's carefully arranged routines, his meticulous attention to every detail, the comfort he derived from knowing that everything was in its proper place – from knowing that everything (and everyone) *had* a proper place – all of this, even down to the standardised perfection of his features; these were all soothing to her and infinitely reassuring.

But she had found, during these two honeymoon years of her marriage, that they could also be tiring, not to say exhausting. There were days when she longed to stay in bed and perhaps eat breakfast there – something Kareem would never countenance, because breakfast always created crumbs, and the mere idea of crumbs on the sheets, of stray food particles insinuating themselves, unseen, into folds and creases and lying there, potentially for hours, polluting their sleep space, was too terrible to contemplate. Then there were afternoons when she would put down a book she had been reading and toy with the idea of just leaving it there. Once or twice she had done so, but within moments of Kareem returning home from the office, she found the book had disappeared, back to the shelf where, admittedly, she was easily able to find it again thanks to his logical, alphabetised system.

She shook off these recollections as the car that had collected her from the airport drew nearer to the spires of Oxford's centre. The main points to remember – and she was assiduous about remembering them – were that Kareem was a decent man, with good values and solid ethics. He had a charm, a sense of humour that she had not found to be widespread in other Arab men she knew, and she enjoyed the way that he could make their friends – even her parents – laugh over dinner or tea parties. This way he had with her parents and the approval and attention that Lamia had felt emanating from Reema since her marriage had also been gratifying. And Kareem was liberal. She still kept an office in Amman, at her father's headquarters and, if anything, he was always overly concerned to ask her about what exactly was happening with her family's businesses. He had many such flashes of consideration, she realised, and so many of her friends' husbands did not. She liked having the office there, it gave her a focus. She did not want to become one of those women with nothing better to do after seeing their husbands off to work than to frequent the gym and have coffee afterwards. She would maintain her desk until she had children, at least, and then her life would be devoted to them. She sensed, sometimes, that life was made of something more, that there was a spark which could elevate it to another plane; she had, in fact, felt something of this during those early days of Kareem's attentions. That feeling had left her some time ago, eroded by routines and habits and familiarity, but she could still summon it up sometimes, when she focused hard, but she remembered to do so less and less often.

Outside, the late morning sunlight was soft and unobtrusive, very unlike the glare of Amman. Lamia ventured to remove her sunglasses as the car pulled to a stop outside the hotel. Even without proper shops, parts of this city were quite beautiful and she was further pleased to remember that she would not have to share a room with Tala this time, because Tala was bringing a friend and the friend would share with her, leaving Lamia to luxuriate alone in her crisply-sheeted bed.

In the café where they had just finished breakfast, Tala slipped her phone back into her pocket. 'A text from Lamia,' she explained. 'She arrived at the hotel.'

'Should we go and meet her?'

Tala shook her head. 'Count on an hour for her to shower and change. Plenty of time for you to go to the bookstore. Go ahead, I'll wait for you here.'

Leyla stood up. 'What will you do? Have a coffee?'

Tala nodded, drew two magazines from her bag and smiled.

'I want to read your stories again.'

'Then I'm definitely going,' Leyla smiled and left. Tala watched her weaving through the tables, her gait a little awkward and shy, as though she sensed she was being watched. Leyla stepped outside and glanced back to wave. The sun fell on her now, burnishing her skin, gleaming on her hair. Tala raised a hand in acknowledgment and then quickly looked down.

She had been trying hourly to ensure that this new friendship with Leyla remained such, to be certain that it would not slip out of the careful grasp of her fingers and into the darker chambers of her heart. That had happened to her once or twice before, with women she had felt an instant connection with, and somehow the friendship had tipped over into something more, something wrong and Tala felt it was just a flaw or a need she had to correct in herself. Certainly she had no wish to negotiate the viscous swamps of despair and self-disgust that had accompanied those times in her life. Yet now Leyla had begun to fill a space in Tala's heart, a desire for intimacy, for friendship. She had felt Hani fill that space once, not so long ago. For he too was a good friend to her, someone with whom she laughed and from whom she learned. But they had been mostly apart for the past few months – he working in Amman, she in London – and when she had found Leyla insinuating herself into her daily thoughts, Tala had told herself that it was not wrong for her to want a close friend. But she also knew that it was essential that she stopped noticing the sunlight on her hair and the nuances of her eye colour; that she cease communicating with her constantly and silently with the heightened intimacy of exchanged glances.

She looked at the stories lying on her lap. It was these stories, which Leyla had given to her so tentatively after the theatre, which had begun, too easily, to weaken the taut pull of her resolve. The stories were exceptionally good, which was not a surprise as much as a pleasure. They had vastly diverse settings and tones, but both were tales of love almost found but ultimately lost – a classic theme which was handled lightly and delicately, yet which evoked in Tala a mood of such profoundly delicious regret that it had permeated all her responses for hours afterwards. And here, in the vibrant restaurant, as she began to read the words again, Tala tasted again the light, delicious mist of melancholy upon her tongue.

She considered Leyla, concentrated on how she could evoke emotions and sensations simply by placing words on a page. Why did she do it? It seemed entirely natural that Leyla should possess such ability, and yet so unlikely. She was so quiet most of the time, so self-effacing. And yet on these pages were intelligence, expressiveness, passion.

When her telephone rang again, she could only, in her cloud of wishful imaginings, comprehend that it might be Leyla, and she snatched it up eagerly.

'My darling,' the voice said. She blinked.

'Hani!'

'Is this a bad time?'

She reassured him that she had only been reading.

'Not contracts I hope?'

She glanced guiltily at the pages that lay open before her. 'No. Not contracts. How are you, Hani?'

'Missing you.'

'Me too,' she replied.

'Really?'

She wished that he would not push the question like that.

'Of course. How's my favourite city?' she asked, falling back on irony to cover her embarrassment.

Amman was the same, he told her, nothing ever changed. She listened to his account of the internal battles he was waging in his government department, and the dispiriting baseness of the politics dampened even the relaxed cadences of Hani's voice. He changed the subject deftly, trying to fire her enthusiasm, to the camping weekend he had taken in Wadi Rum.

'It was stunning, Tala,' he said. 'Just the desert, the stars, the amazing rock formations. Really, we have to do this together some time.'

'I'd like to,' she said. Perhaps that was what she needed. To stop focusing her attention on the parts of her home country that she abhorred – the navel-gazing society, the tradition-obsessed mindset – and to simply enjoy the natural beauty. She pictured the wild desert landscape of Wadi Rum at night, imagined how the overarching beauty could inspire and impress. It had been fifteen years since she had been there.

'Let's do it when I come back for the wedding,' she said decisively. 'It'll be a crazy few weeks. We can get away for a couple of days.'

'That'd be great,' he replied, and she could hear the pleasure in his voice. She was able to lift emotion from him so easily. She frowned.

'I miss you, Hani,' she said.

'Want me to come see you?'

'No, don't,' she said. 'You can't leave work anyway. And I'm busy here. We'll see each other soon.'

'I know,' he said. 'I love you.'

'Me too,' she replied quickly and turned off the phone.

Putting the stories firmly back into her bag, she ordered another coffee, picked up a newspaper that had been left behind at a neighbouring table and sat back, with some determination, to read about what was happening in the Middle East.

Lamia was still in her robe after a long soak in the bathtub when she heard Tala knocking insistently on her door. Her sister held her in a long hug before planting a kiss on her cheek. Lamia smiled self-conciously and pulled back. As usual, she was slightly unnerved by Tala's openness, by the hearty enthusiasm of her self-expression. Such excited physicality, such verve, did not come as easily or naturally to Lamia – she was quieter, a silent observer, who eschewed extremes of emotion or activity.

'You look amazing,' Tala said. It was true. Lamia had always been beautiful, but there was an aura about her today that made her even more striking. She had lost some weight too, and that had sharpened the high planes of her cheekbones and made her soulful eyes seem even larger. Tala turned and led the way into the bedroom, where she turned down the widescreen television which was beaming out pictures of the latest strife in the Middle East.

'Did you see that?' Tala asked. 'More trouble in the West Bank.'

Lamia knew that she should be interested, but could not overcome the fact that she was faint with hunger. She had missed breakfast, having left at an ungodly hour from Amman that morning, and though she would have liked to have skipped lunch, she felt compelled to have a salad at least.

'Are we going out to eat?' she asked.

'Leyla and I thought Italian. She felt like pasta.'

'I don't do carbs,' Lamia said, alarmed.

'Why?'

'I feel better without them,' she said.

'What do you eat? Too much protein isn't good for you,' Tala said.

Lamia resisted the urge to bite her thumbnail. She was inordinately conscious that Tala had only been in her space for two minutes and was already making her feel defensive.

'I don't eat red meat, remember?' she said.

In the brief silence that ensued, Tala reminded herself that Lamia was old enough to decide for herself what kind of diet she wanted to follow. She had forgotten about the meat, though. When she was perhaps fourteen, Lamia had been at her friend's house on the outskirts of Amman, and had watched as the new neighbours moved in, bringing with them an old tradition of slaughtering a lamb to bestow luck on a new house. Lamia had watched, horrified, as the clueless animal was led out of a pick-up truck and onto the front patio. She had meant to look away before the killing took place, but with indecent haste, a knife had been produced and the throat slit open. She had stared, open-mouthed, the bile rising in her stomach as several pairs of hands were dipped into the warm, dripping blood, and signs were painted on the door to ward off the evil eye. She had wept, and her friend's mother had laughed and explained to her the tradition and its long practice, but Lamia had not eaten meat since.

Over lunch, Tala watched Lamia as she precisely, methodically, picked out a few stray tubes of pasta that had escaped onto her plate, amid slices of roasted vegetables.

'I thought we could go to the Ashmolean Museum this afternoon,' Tala said, to prevent herself from commenting on her sister's picky eating habits. 'Before our meeting.'

'We need to shop,' was Lamia's sharp reply. 'For your wedding.'

'The museum has a shop,' Tala said, instantly regretting the sarcasm. It was too easy to make fun of her sister and she wished she could control the impulse to rile her all the time.

Lamia pushed back her plate and sighed.

'Lamia, you used to study here, didn't you?' Leyla asked quickly

Lamia nodded but offered no further details, because she was watching Tala lift a forkful of her own food and place it in Leyla's

mouth. It struck her as unnecessarily intimate, as well as unhygien-
ic. She had tried to do that once with Kareem, to offer him a taste
of something she had truly enjoyed, but he had declined and spent
the ensuing minutes explaining the armies of germs that would have
swarmed onto the fork from her mouth and that she now, in a supposedly caring gesture, wanted to transfer to him. His earnest explanation certainly had removed any hint of romanticism from the idea
and Lamia had never tried it again. She looked away from the girls
opposite her, for Tala's head was bent too close to Leyla's and they
were giggling about something that she had missed. Tala looked up,
and shifted her position away from Leyla slightly, casually.

'You know, Leyla's going to be a great writer one day. One day
we'll walk into any Oxford bookstore or library and be able to see
her books.'

Tala was looking at the girl with such pride, in a way she had
never looked at Lamia herself.

'That's nice,' Lamia said, trying to make an effort, but Tala just
rolled her eyes.

'Hey, Leyla,' Tala said with a grin. 'Maybe you can publish an
edition with pictures in it. For my sister.'

Lamia began to gather her bag and coat in preparation for leaving. With Tala in such a flippant mood, and after all the insults she
had endured over lunch, there was no chance that Lamia would ac-
company those two to dredge through another museum. There was
a spa in the hotel where she could while away the time before their
meeting with the college Dean, and anyway, Kareem would be placing his usual call after lunch to check on her and see how she was.

Walking together through the streets that separated the old colleges of the town, Leyla looked around, taking in the elegant, stone
buildings upon which smudges of afternoon sunlight were smeared
like streaks of amber pollen.

'That sweet city with her dreaming spires' said Tala. Leyla looked at her, surprised.

'That's a Matthew Arnold quote,' she said. 'How did you know it?'

Tala raised an eyebrow. 'Do writers have a monopoly on reading poetry?'

Leyla smiled in acknowledgement.

'Look, I'm sorry if Lamia is a bit hard to take,' said Tala, changing the subject. 'I don't understand anything about her any more. The way she spends her time, her views on things. Her marriage. It's exactly that kind of conservative, controlling relationship that I've always wanted to avoid at all costs.'

'So your fiancé's not like that?' Leyla asked. Tala had spoken very little about Hani when they were together, and Leyla had found herself having to remember to ask about him.

'Hani? No. He's an Arab, born and brought up in Jordan, but he's not like the rest. He's very gentle. Very kind. I know exactly who he is. There's no game playing.'

'He sounds wonderful,' Leyla smiled, and she tried to dispel the touch of disappointment that she felt at Tala's glowing appraisal of her fiancé. It was wrong and as Tala's friend she should be thrilled. But then Tala's own eyes were dark and reflective as she looked off towards the church, from which a delicate chime floated across to them, naming the hour.

'He is. He really is,' said Tala, uncomfortable suddenly. 'At least, I can't find anything wrong with him,' she joked. But her brows were drawn in, and her smile melted away too quickly.

'Why are you trying?' Leyla asked. It was a bold step, and Leyla was still a little surprised she had taken it, but it clearly touched a raw spot of some kind, for Tala turned away a little, folding her arms about her.

'It's four,' Leyla said. 'You should go to your meeting with Lamia. I'll meet you back at the hotel later.'

Tala nodded and they walked together to the main road, where

Tala hailed a cab and hurried into it, pausing only briefly to wish Leyla a pleasant afternoon. Leyla watched the cab drive off until it turned out of sight, but Tala did not glance back to wave.

The fork-sharing and general cosiness over lunch had left Lamia quite nauseated. During the meeting about the charity event (which seemed to drag on forever) she kept her sunglasses on, using the dark lenses as a cover through which she watched Tala as she spoke with the Dean. Her sister looked better than she had in a while, Lamia thought, sort of healthy and glowing, although it wouldn't kill her to do something with her hair occasionally. But she didn't have Lamia's sense of style or fashion, nor was she quite skinny enough, and as far as Lamia could ascertain, her fledgling business hadn't made money yet. And yet she seemed to appear permanently pleased with herself. Frankly, why she was cavorting around Oxford for a weekend with some girl when she had wedding preparations and a fiancé to attend to, was beyond her. Lamia was not sure whether she liked Leyla. She was too quiet, too knowing, her eyes were always probing, she felt, and she was clearly a bad influence on Tala, enticing her to museums and libraries when she should be shopping.

It was only a further annoyance to Lamia, then, that in the taxi home, Tala's conversation consisted of nothing but Leyla and how wonderful and talented she was. Lamia opened the window to conquer her light-headedness.

'What's the matter?' Tala asked.

'Nothing. Just a bit dizzy.'

'Because you ate a lettuce leaf at lunch. You must be starving. We'll have dinner…'

'No. I don't want dinner. I want an early night.'

'Maybe I'll do the same,' Tala said, and Lamia noted that her eyes flickered to the window from which she stared out with a slight smile on her face. What was so exciting about an early night? And with a girlfriend? Lamia knew, of course, she was not stupid. She had noticed this happen to Tala once before, with a girl whose name Lamia could not even recall, back when they were at university together and had shared a house. It must have been eight years ago, but Lamia remembered the signs – the glow in Tala's face, her wistful looks from windows, her secret smiles, and most obviously, her inability to stop talking about the girl in question.

'How did Leyla become a writer?' Lamia asked conversationally and she closed the window and sat back to listen. The more Lamia nodded and encouraged, the more emboldened Tala felt to speak. It was the downfall of love, Lamia thought wistfully, that it inspired the lover to toss away any shred of caution just to obtain the pure, desperate pleasure of talking about the beloved. And Lamia was better versed in this weakness than many. When she was twenty years old she had fallen insanely in love with a young man who worked as a manager for the manufacturing section of her father's business. This love created a new universe for Lamia, a previously untasted world, in which she existed far above the general thrust and push of daily life. She ate when directed to, and every night lay down in the cool solitude of her bed to enjoy only the idea of him. She passed whole days at work with the smiling docility of an idiot, without knowing what she was doing or why. She delighted in the ice-hard, pale blue dawn that broke each morning across the ramshackle, disorganised buildings of Amman, knowing that, across the tiny city, he was watching the sunrise with her. He was intelligent and kind, with a rare integrity that made him feel no shame that he worked for a living and could not yet own a business. This disadvantage, the disparity in their financial situations, could perhaps have been overcome with time and patience and insistence on her part. But he was also Muslim, and that, Lamia knew, was nothing less than impossible. He told her that his family would not accept her if she remained a Christian, and she knew that hers would never countenance a conversion to Islam. They had continued their affair in secret for three months, and by the end of that time, Lamia had felt herself so inflated with passion that she knew she would implode if she could not speak of it to anyone. Tala was in the States, Zina was in a Swiss boarding school, and only Reema was there, in Amman, at the end of every day, waiting, prodding, gently opening out the reticence that she could sniff inside her daughter, like the scent of a lily dying in the darkness. At last, Lamia had confided in her mother, and Reema had listened with a consoling hand on her child's back, and understanding in her eyes. And the next morning, when Lamia went to the office, she found that the young man was gone. He had been fired, and she realised later, so strongly advised that he should not see her that he never tried to contact her again, even in secret.

By the time they arrived back at the hotel, the final scrap of evidence was offered up to Lamia's scrutiny when Tala confessed that she was nervous about the wedding. Not about the menu or her dress, but about whether it was the right move.

'All brides have jitters,' Lamia told her, walking up the steps to the lobby. She paused and looked directly into Tala's eyes. They looked tired and flickered away from Lamia's gaze. Lamia felt a momentary pang of pity for her sister.

'You won't find anyone like Hani ever again,' Lamia told her. 'And he adores you.'

'Yes,' said Tala.

'You just need a good night's sleep,' Lamia said kindly. 'Everything will look different in the morning.'

Chapter 7

EVERYTHING ALREADY LOOKED DIFFERENT this evening, Tala thought, as she walked into the hotel room that she and Leyla were sharing. When they had checked in that morning, the sun that flooded the cream walls and reproduction furniture had lent an air of light, of innocence, to the double bed sitting squarely in the centre of the room. But now, the summer light beyond the windows had faded under the dusk, and the lamp light in the room, together with the music – a sensual, Arabic voice – that issued from the CD player lent the whole place an air of romance that was not appropriate, Tala felt, but that was inviting all the same.

She could hear Leyla in the bathroom, could see the crack of light beneath the door. She rapped on it lightly.

'I'm back,' she called. 'Make sure you're decent!'

She winced. Why had she said that? Why imply the possibility of being indecent? Anyway, they were two girls together, what would it matter if Leyla appeared in her bra?

And so Tala reached into the mini bar for a bottle of water and sat awkwardly on the edge of the bed, trying without success to erase the image of Leyla in her underwear from her mind.

Leyla emerged from the bathroom somewhat tense. She had missed Tala's company for the couple of hours that she had been at the meeting, but as soon as she had heard her confident knock on the bathroom door, the announcement that she was back, Leyla suddenly felt a nervous energy clutch her stomach and was unable to think of anything normal to say. If she was to be honest with herself, the idea of sharing the bed with Tala, of sharing the night, had been looming in her mind, adding an unseemly edge of excitement to her afternoon's activities, and yet leaving a knot in her stomach. Because the excitement was all on her side. And it would be – should be – unrequited. Tala was getting married, and she loved someone. Someone else. But the emotions coursing through her veins would not turn off at a command, and Leyla knew she would have to get through the proximity, the long reach of dark hours together by keeping herself held in and quiet, so that Tala would never even be able to guess at the feelings that were hidden carefully away. She opened the bathroom door, and stepped out into the room, trying to appear natural and relaxed.

Tala looked up at Leyla, who was standing before her, waiting, trying to judge her mood, her feelings, as they both often did now, without words. Her hair was still damp from the shower. And she was dressed, but in a sleeveless t-shirt that clung distractingly to her stomach and chest and which showed the lean line of muscles in her arms. Tala stifled a sigh, and looked away, prompting Leyla to ask her what was wrong. She couldn't think of an answer, so she stayed quiet.

'Didn't the meeting go well?' Leyla asked, stepping forward. Tala leaned back slightly.

'It went fine, thanks.'

Why did she keep moving forward like that? She was just concerned, obviously.

'What's wrong, Tala?'

'Nothing, I'm fine.' Tala shook herself. 'Are you hungry?'

'A little. Do you want to go out?'

'If you'd like to.'

She could feel Leyla sit down beside her on the bed, could feel her eyes watching her, wondering, evaluating. But Tala could not look back. She felt strange, removed from herself, and she did not want to talk about it.

'Why don't I just order room service for us?' the girl suggested.

'Okay'.

And now, instead of getting up and using the phone across the room, by the chair, Leyla reached across Tala for the receiver that lay next to her, by the bed. Why did she have to do that? Tala wondered. The sudden, fresh scent of Leyla's skin and hair distracted her and she found herself staring at the tanned, brown arm that stretched before her, and the long fingers that closed around the telephone. Tala felt herself lean forward, just slightly, felt her lips touch the arm, at the valley of the elbow, touch the cool, clean taste of Leyla's skin against her mouth. She felt the arm tense slightly, but it did not draw away. She saw the phone drop back onto the table, felt Leyla's other hand come up to caress her head and her cheek and she closed her eyes against any other thought, so that there was only this sensation, the touch of Leyla's hand on her face, the recent memory of her skin still burning her mouth.

'Look at me,' Leyla was whispering. 'Look.'

She looked. But the movement brought their faces too close together, and Tala's eyes held the crushed liquidity of Leyla's gaze for a long moment, but then she dropped her glance down to the girl's mouth, the lips slightly parted, and she felt herself move forward again, felt her own lips brush Leyla's softly, very softly, a touch that she felt in every part of her body, arousing a desire she had denied at every moment. She pressed harder against Leyla, covering her mouth with her own till she felt the delicate trace of her tongue against hers. Softly, she moaned, a sound she had no control over, but she did not speak, for there was nothing more to say.

All she could feel was Leyla's hands on her, slipping gently beneath her shirt, caressing her back and sides and sliding up to her breasts, cupping them, her thumb touching the nipples that strained stiffly against her bra. And Leyla's mouth on her neck, weaving a soft line with her lips up to Tala's ear where she could hear her breathing, quick and breathless. Leyla's fingers were coaxing open the buttons of Tala's shirt now, pulling it down over her shoulders, pulling down her bra, and Tala fell back onto the bed, with Leyla on top of her, her tongue tracing a path down to her breasts, her own hands moving over Leyla's back and down, caressing a silken line between her thighs. Now Leyla gave an audible sigh, an intake of breath as Tala reached the centre of her, and together they began to move against each other in a rhythm that neither had to search for.

Pacing the uninspired carpet of her hotel room, Lamia listened to Reema's voice, surprisingly clear on the mobile she held pressed to her ear.

'I hope you got her colourful clothes?' Reema demanded.

'Tala thinks grey *is* a colour. And they got bored of shopping.'

It was a calculated move, this last sentence. Lamia bit at her thumbnail as she paced, glancing up at the muted television for support. Reema caught the reference at once.

'They?'

'Her friend is here with her. Leyla.'

'The Indian Jewess?'

Lamia frowned, confused. 'The Indian. I didn't know she was Jewish. Anyway, I guess it's nice for Tala to have such a close friend.'

'Hmmm,' replied Reema. 'Good thing she's coming back soon for the wedding.'

'That's the other thing...' Lamia paused, hesitating. She could contrive to convince herself that she had only thrown Leyla's name into the conversation by accident, not knowing it might concern her mother. But this next step would be a more active decision on her part, to give away information that Tala had shared with her confidentially. As a sister.

'Lamia?' coaxed Reema, at the other end of the phone. 'You know sometimes Tala needs help to see what's best for her.' Lamia could hear an extended exhalation of breath, pictured her mother in her dressing room in Amman, smoking, waiting. Waiting.

Lamia sat down on her bed. 'She said she wants to stay in London a while longer.'

Lamia could feel her mother's eyes narrow. 'She did that during her second engagement – or was it the first? And she never came back for the wedding!'

'I'm sure it's not exactly like that, Mama.'

But there was no reply. 'Mama?' Lamia tried again, a little panicked now, but nothing came except the click of the connection being cut with a soft finality. Tapping her heel up and down as she sat, Lamia felt a sudden suffusion of righteousness rise up inside her – for she was doing the right thing to save Tala from herself. Just as her mother had done for Lamia years before. Lamia could see now that her young, immature passion would have had little chance of lasting – such firecracker emotions rarely did – and that once the love had ceased to consume every part of her being, she would have been left fighting the ancient, wearing battles of Muslim against Christian. Although at the time she had been convinced that she had both the stomach and the armour for this fight, Reema had assured her that she did not, and then gave her no possible chance to try, and in retrospect, there was little Lamia could do for her own peace of mind but believe that her mother's words were true.

Tala awoke from dreams suffused with warmth and heat and drowsy intimacy, and into a morning of harsh light and the insistent ring of her cell phone. Gently, she drew her hand away from Leyla's sleeping form and reached for the phone, sitting up. She knew who it was, and moved quickly towards the bathroom as she answered.

'Hi Hani. Yes, no, I'm fine. No, everything's fine, I just woke up, that's all.'

She heard Leyla shift in the bed, knew she was awake and listening. Swiftly, Tala slipped on her robe.

'Listen, can I call you later? When I'm up?' She nodded, relieved. 'OK, thanks Hani.'

And then came the ending to the call that she had been trying to avoid just now. But he loved her, and he couldn't help saying it and she couldn't blame him, and when she heard his strong, happy voice, she felt a rush of feeling towards him.

'I love you too,' she whispered. She hung up, washed over with guilt towards him, but also towards the girl lying in her bed. She rinsed her face, studiously avoiding its reflection in the mirror and brushed her teeth quickly, thinking about the night before. When she emerged from the bathroom, Leyla's head was still on her pillow, but her eyes, so uncertain, were on her. Tala went to the bed and sat down, leaning to kiss the girl's shoulder.

'Have you ever done this before?' Leyla asked her, shifting up in the bed.

Tala looked away. 'Slept with a woman while my fiancé makes wedding preparations?' She considered a moment then shook her head. 'No. Never done that before.'

'You know what I meant.'

Tala took in an audible breath. She disliked being forced into a place where she had to remember things, feelings, that she only recollected, infrequently, in the floating suspension of dreams. Things she had never spoken of openly to anyone. But she supposed that if ever there was a person who deserved to hear the things she preferred to keep private, it was this clear-eyed woman lying naked in her hotel room bed.

'When I was eighteen,' Tala said. 'I fell madly in love with a girl, my first year in college.' She could feel her cheeks flush crimson with the force of actually saying the words. 'It lasted a few, wonderful, months. I never knew I could feel so..alive,' she stammered. 'So complete.'

'Until now, obviously,' said Leyla, dryly. Tala smiled and leaned in to kiss her hair, burying her face there, breathing in the soft scent of it, until her heart should stop racing quite so hard. Leyla's hand came up to hold her head. She heard Leyla speak, quietly.

'What happened?'

'I broke it off. I was in pieces, but I told myself it was for the best. That I was away from home and lonely and...' Tala stopped talking and pulled back, pulled away.

'And now?'

'This is not a way to live, Leyla,' she said. 'It's not easy. It's not acceptable.'

'We didn't break any rules last night, Tala.'

'We did where I come from. Nobody lives like this. Not openly.'

Leyla sighed. 'You live in the West now.'

Tala looked down, her voice hoarse. 'Yes, but I don't think it's acceptable to cheat on your fiancé anywhere in the world.'

The silence that sat in the room felt profound, with nothing to break it but the occasional passing car. Tala saw Leyla nod and close her eyes. Carefully, she moved closer to her on the bed, cradling the girl in her arms and kissing her head and face.

'What happens now?' Leyla whispered.

'I don't know,' Tala said, kissing away a tear that had escaped from Leyla's tightly shut lids. 'I really don't know.'

Chapter 8

THERE WAS VERY LITTLE TALK between them in the car
back to London. Even after they had dropped Lamia off in
Sloane Street to shop, they both sat without speaking, the silence
resting between them like an uninvited guest . Tala's hand instinctively went to Leyla's and she held it with a kind of desperation.

'Stay the night with me,' Tala said, quietly. 'Please.'

'And then what?'

Tala shook her head. There was a blank wall in her mind where
the answer to that question ought to be. Leyla shifted in her seat
and leaned to kiss Tala's mouth.

'Please stay,' Tala asked again. 'I can't be away from you tonight.'

They pulled up outside her house.

'It'll just make it all worse,' said Leyla.

Nevertheless, she opened the car door and got out, watching
while Tala placed the key in the lock and swung open the heavy
front door. She had stopped thinking for a while now, had been
unable to focus on anything but Tala's scent, her taste, the memories
of the night before. It was a physical need pushing at her, and Leyla
knew there were so many things to consider, so many possibilities to

talk about, and yet, as soon as Tala closed the front door, she found herself crushed against her, kissing her with a passion that had no reason or control. All she could feel was the tension of Tala's legs against and between her own, the touch of her lips on Tala's neck, as they staggered together into the living room, where the sofa lay so wide and empty.

Tala couldn't have said what it was she heard that caused her to suddenly hold back as Leyla was pulling her down towards her. Perhaps a creak, the way that floorboard in the hallway outside always creaked when your foot hit it a certain way. But she stood up, her hand still entwined with Leyla's, and turned just in time to see her mother standing in the doorway.

After she had calmed down, Reema had called Lamia back and they had spoken at length, after which Reema had at once formulated a plan and woken up early to take the flight to London that very morning, accompanied by reinforcements, including, as usual, her faithful housekeeper, Rani. It was Lamia who, of all her children, at least took the time to really communicate with her, to convey to her myriad details, precise images, thoughtful deductions. It made for more interesting conversation than Tala's quick overviews, or Zina's accusatory complaints. And among the deductions that Lamia had made within a few hours of her arrival in Oxford, was that her elder sister was once again in thrall to some unknown person, and that this person was not Hani, and far worse, was not a man at all.

It was immediately clear to Reema that she had arrived just in time. She took in the little tableau before her: Leyla on the sofa, Tala standing above her, clearly surprised. The sudden shift which they made away from each other was further evidence, if any were needed, that something untoward was in the air. Sweeping in, Reema kissed the air by her daughter's cheek, brushing off her stuttered shock that Reema was in London, and shook Leyla's hand. They all stood together for a tense moment, polite and awkward, until the

telephone rang. A slow smile broke across Reema's face and she nodded at Tala to answer it.

Unbalanced, confused, Tala reached for the phone and flicked it
on. It was Hani. As they exchanged greetings, she tried to recover
herself, for she could hardly believe the poor timing of her mother's
surprise arrival from Amman.

'I just walked in from Oxford,' Tala told him, trying to negotiate
an early end to the call. Her eyes flickered between her mother and
Leyla, who were speaking, exchanging pleasantries, which she was
intent on lip-reading in case the conversation should deteriorate.

'I know,' Hani replied.

Tala frowned, her attention scattered. 'What? How do you
know?'

'I can see you.' She could hear a smile in Hani's voice, and before any concrete thought could trouble her mind, her stomach
dropped.

'What do you mean?' Tala asked, desperately. 'Where are you?'

'Right here,' and she immediately became aware of a large shape
lingering outside in the hallway, a shape that solidified into something, someone recognisable as it took two steps into the room.
Hani.

'Your mother suggested it. A surprise for you.'

His voice was suddenly rich and real after the tinny distortion of
the phone. He stood looking at her, tall, smiling, his eyes filled with
excitement and adoration. His arms were open to her now, and automatically she moved forward, as she was required to, as she would
have done without thinking had Leyla not been standing next to
her. She was wrapped in a hug, in the honest, familiar scent of him,
which enveloped her for some thirty long seconds.

'I missed you, Tala,' Hani was telling her. 'Now we can go back
to Amman together.'

Reema sat down and smiled at Leyla, a smile of companionship and conspiracy that they two should be witnessing this beautiful reunion of lovers. Leyla smiled back; she was smiling, an intense grimace, as though her life relied upon it, and she too sat down, collapsed down, into the forgiving leather of the sofa behind her. He was kissing Tala now, she could not help but see, on her head, on her mouth and holding her again. Leyla looked at Reema, for she had to look away from the couple in the doorway, and as the older woman reached for the cigarette lighter, Leyla imagined her response if it were she who was hugging and kissing her daughter on the other side of the room. She would kill me, Leyla thought, wildly. With her curved, manicured fingers she would hold the flaming palm tree lighter to my clothes and incinerate me. Then they would kill their daughter. An honour killing. She had read about them. It wouldn't be a crime, it would be a duty, a necessity, a cause for celebration.

'They're so in love, it brings tears to my eyes,' Reema confided, letting out a stream of cigarette smoke that seemed to solidify in the turgid air between them. Then she reached for a tissue and dabbed gently at the side of her eyes.

Aware of Leyla's agony, Tala tried delicately to pull as far away from Hani as possible without actually having him notice. She took off her jacket, folding it carefully, taking her time, avoiding the moment when she must sit beside her fiancé and accept his touch of her hand, the way he always touched her when they were close together. She felt Reema's intense, close interest as she observed them; she felt it like a cold breath on her neck. Her mother's triumphant air had not escaped her either. She was certain that Hani had been made a pawn in one of Reema's unsavoury games, but the disgust she felt at this was offset by her fiancé's genuine excitement at seeing her. But her real concern was for Leyla. She was suffering, Tala could tell, and she could not think of a way to ease it.

It was obvious to Leyla that Hani's eyes sought only Tala, that his whole being gravitated towards her, happily, willingly, helplessly. This made his immediate attention towards Leyla herself all the more remarkable and kind – he sat opposite her and spent several minutes enquiring about her background, her work, the general terms of her life. Under the warmth and openness of his gaze, Leyla began to feel less lost, less panicked.

'Oxford must have been beautiful,' he said, genuinely interested. 'The buildings. The river.'

'It was wonderful,' Leyla replied, with a stab of guilt. She would not, could not look directly at Tala. Hani smiled and reached for Tala's hand, which held his for a moment. She was grateful for his interest in Leyla; it was typical of his kindness and openness, and she felt guilty towards him, that she was hiding from him certain feelings; that he knew so much less of her than he realised. With relief, she turned to the doorway where Rani stood with the news that lunch was on the table.

Leyla got up, quickly, sensing an opportunity to fashion a hasty exit, for she could not imagine having to sit through a meal with the woman she was in love with, her terrifying mother and her kind fiancé.

'I really have to go, I...'

'I won't hear of it,' Reema interrupted firmly. 'A quick bite. We can all get to know each other.'

With assertive elegance, she blocked off the door to the hallway and ushered them all into the cavernous formal dining room, where four places were set at one end of a table that was long enough to seat a small banquet. Reema indicated their places, which she had chosen strategically, positioning Leyla next to herself, so she could fully enjoy the view of Hani and Tala opposite, together.

'This looks amazing,' Hani said, looking at the food. 'I've been learning to cook myself, you know.'

'Why?' Tala asked.

'Because you don't,' Reema answered. 'And I tried to teach her,' she assured Hani, as if she were offering him a mule with which she had done her best but which retained a stubborn temperament all the same. 'I know we have cooks and staff, but one has to know what should be going on in the kitchen, if you want to give the right orders.'

'That's how my boss justifies giving me the worst jobs to do, Aunty,' Hani laughed. 'He tells me its good experience.'

'Hani works in the Jordanian government,' Reema told Leyla. She was pleased that her son-in-law (for she already considered him as such) had underscored the value of her cooking analogy, but could not understand why he would draw attention to the fact that he worked under so many people. He didn't need to work at all, except to watch over his father's wealth, but since he insisted on it, Reema made a note to train him out of his habit of self-deprecation after the wedding, or to make sure he rose up the ranks more quickly. Although exactly how far he could go would be hindered by two facts, ironically the same two that made him such a marvellous catch as a husband for Tala – that he was Christian, and that he was Palestinian. Never in Jordan's history had a Christian made it to the post of Prime Minister. But perhaps Foreign Minister? Reema brightened. It was unlikely, but not, she calculated, impossible. Particularly if he could be persuaded to stop drawing attention to the fact that he was of Palestinian origin. Although the vast majority of Jordan's population was Palestinian, there was always underlying resentment from the true Jordanians, Reema thought bitterly.

'Hani works in the foreign office,' Tala added. It was the first comment she had made directly to Leyla since her mother's arrival, and she allowed her eyes to rest on the girl opposite for a few moments, during which she tried to convey all the remorse, uncertainty and concern that she felt. Leyla looked away, to Hani.

'Does that cover relations with Israel?'

'Yes, it does.'

'Must be hard work.'

'The hardest,' he smiled. 'But I have hope we can come to resolution in the end. The Palestinians, I mean.'

There he went again, Reema noted with annoyance. He worked for Jordan, not Palestine.

'How can you have hope?' Leyla asked, a question which was less a political concern than a direct articulation of the crushing sensation in her chest. 'Half the Palestinians don't want Israel to even exist,' she continued, 'and the other half are being trampled by Israeli settlements and tanks anyway.'

There was a moment of silence, which Reema had geared up to fill, when Hani spoke quietly.

'If I don't have hope, then I might as well give up.' He took a drink of water. 'As soon as the more radical Arabs accept that Israel does exist, that it's not going to disappear, that they can't and shouldn't be trying to blow it up, then we can move to the next step.'

'How many models of democracy do we have in the Middle East?' Tala asked suddenly. 'Israel isn't perfect but it's the closest. Maybe we can learn something.'

'What do you want to learn?' Reema interrupted. 'How to shoot children?'

'I'm not defending Israel's actions, far from it,' Tala replied, grateful for the chance to snipe at her mother, even over the wrong cause. 'But let's not forget that our own Arab leaders have often not treated their own people well either.'

'That doesn't make what Israel does right...' Hani said quietly.

'I don't think that's Tala's point,' Leyla said. 'Is it?'

For the first time, they looked at each other.

'I don't know what I did,' Reema growled, 'to give birth to such an Arab-hater.'

Tala flinched slightly, then threw her mother a disgusted glance that focused onto Reema all her anger, all her confusion, all of her distaste and dissatisfaction for everything that was happening

– from the politics of their region, to the subterfuge of Hani's visit, to her mother's refusal to stop meddling in Tala's personal life. Hani put a hand on Tala's back, and Leyla saw that the movement reached something within her; that it stimulated a pause, a breath.

'Aunty,' Hani said, his tone polite but firm. 'Your daughter is one of the proudest Palestinians I know.'

The boy was clearly head over heels in love, Reema thought. She was irritated beyond belief, but she would not risk arguing back until the marriage contract had been signed. The following silence held only the alternately crisp and liquid sounds of tense mastication.

'The food is delicious,' Leyla murmured at last.

'Do you cook?' Reema asked.

Under the laser gaze, Leyla sat up slightly in her chair. 'Yes. I love food. And cooking.'

'Curries?' Reema enquired.

Tala sighed irritably. 'Why do you assume that someone of Indian descent can only make a curry?' she asked.

'Mama, what is the matter with you today?' demanded Reema. 'We're having a conversation, over lunch, like civilised people do. If you don't want to take part, then don't.'

Hani smiled at Leyla. 'What do you like to cook?'

'It depends on the day.'

'And your mood, right?' Hani asked.

'Yes.'

'For me too.'

Leyla took a breath. He seemed intent on creating links between them, little bonds and commonalities, and she could not stand it. Her throat felt clamped now, the narrow, hard muscles were constricting her breathing, her speech, everything. Behind her, Reema's housekeeper appeared, bearing a silver salver. She deposited a glass of fizzing medication before Reema.

'Are you feeling okay?' asked Reema, the gleam in her eye obscured by the smoke that surrounded her head. Even at mealtimes the biting urge for a cigarette would seek her out, requiring fulfillment, even if Tala and Zina never understood the pressure and always complained.

'Just a headache,' Leyla said hoarsely.

'Here,' Reema offered her the fizzing liquid, sliding the glass across the table. Leyla felt the housekeeper shift uncomfortably behind her.

'No, thank you. I just need the bathroom.'

Reema smiled slightly. 'Upstairs. Ninth door on the left. Rani!'

Rani nodded and hurried to hold the door open for Leyla and waited a polite moment before allowing it to close behind her, after which she glided back to the table and unobtrusively slid the tainted medicine back towards Reema's plate.

The bathroom itself only increased the overwrought feeling which had its roots in Leyla's stomach. All around her, the tiles held a relentless pattern, of yellow and green twisting vines that rose up the walls into a tangled mass that spread around the base of the ceiling. Every small section of space around the basin, each little shelf, was crammed with exquisitely carved soaps, with flowery candles and with perfume bottles. Combined, they created an overpowering and uniquely fake odour of sweetness in the confined space of the room.

Leyla turned the tap on, in case anyone should be listening, and also to enjoy the relief of watching the fresh stream of cold water. She leaned her head, defeated, against the cool glass of the mirror, then splashed her face. The touch of the water was restoring, a relief to her burning anguish. Abruptly, she turned off the tap, dried her face briefly and walked out and down the stairs where she found that Tala was waiting for her. Tala took her hand before she had even stepped into the hallway.

'What are you doing?' Leyla asked.

'Holding your hand.'

'I see. So we each get five minutes of hand-holding? I get a night in Oxford, he gets a night in London?'

She felt Tala pull back slightly, felt her panic at the harshness, felt her turn a little to where Reema's voice rose and fell in the room beyond.

'That's not fair, Leyla…' she began.

'What is fair?' Leyla demanded in a fierce whisper. 'That I make love to you and then make conversation with your fiancé?' She paused, trying to control her voice which had the sound of tears etched into it. 'How can you bear it, Tala?'

'We can't live like this,' Tala said. 'Our families would never understand.'

Perhaps that was true, but Leyla realized that she didn't much care who understood anymore.

Leyla looked down at Tala's hand, entwined with her own, the fingers grasping hers, communicating a need, a desire. She bent her head and touched her lips to it, gently.

'Last night wasn't just an affair. Not for me, anyway,' Leyla looked up, into the eyes that watched her. 'Thanks to you, I know what I want. I want to be with someone who, ten years from now, makes my heart jump when I hear her key in the door.' She hesitated. 'And that someone is you.'

Tala was right there, then, against her, kissing her, and Leyla closed her eyes, relieved to have made sense of this mess, to have found the simple way through. They loved each other, and that was truly what mattered.

'Tala! Are you okay?' Hani's concerned voice, calling from the dining room was a jolt to Leyla, but it had some other, deeper effect on Tala. Leyla felt the hands drop her own, and leave her standing isolated.

'I can't hurt him,' Tala breathed.

'Are you in love with him?' Leyla saw the hesitation, or was it just a pause while she tried a find a way to be kind?

'There are things I love about him.'

Leyla stared at her. Behind them, the grandfather clock began to chime the hour, a sonorous, desolate noise.

'Tala. This is wrong. Tell me you can do this.'

Quickly, she moved forward, clasping Tala's head, kissing her hair, her cheek, but unable to reach the mouth that Tala held away. Leyla pulled back and watched in silence as Tala turned and walked back down the hall before disappearing into the darkened doorway of the dining room. She stood alone in the hallway, and found herself waiting, waiting for Tala to reappear, to realize that her life – her real life – was out here. But all she heard was the commingling of Tala's voice with the others in the room beyond, and the voice was faintly embarrassed, doubtless making excuses for her friend's sudden disappearance. Silently, with a leaden heart, Leyla turned and left the house.

Chapter Nine

Three weeks later

A MMAN WAS COLD, and it was grey. A brief nostalgia for the
humid heat of New York passed over Zina as she closed the window and lay down on the bed, placing a cool hand over her burning
forehead. All the travelling back and forth between New York and
Amman, first for the engagement party and now for the wedding,
hadn't helped her illness. The various tablets that her mother had
been eagerly plying her with over the past two days were evidently
not working, despite the fact that Reema stocked more prescription
medication in her house than most pharmacies. In the dark recesses
of her mind, Zina began to consider the possibility that she did not
have flu after all. Perhaps it was something more sinister. Glandular
fever, or some form of chronic fatigue. Her new and palpable anxiety about this added to the other knots that gathered like a group of
pernicious tentacles in the base of her stomach.

There was a cursory knock on the door before it opened, and
Zina found herself scrambling up from the bed. It was her father.
She had forgotten that personal privacy was a non-existent concept
in her parents' house. It apparently never occurred to her mother

and father that they might ever walk in on any of their children having sex, or smoking a joint, or doing anything that they should not be privy to.

'What are you doing?' he asked. 'Come down, we're having dinner in five minutes.'

'With who? A hundred of our closest friends?' Zina muttered. A glimmer of a smile flickered onto Omar's face.

'It's just us tonight. Your mother, me and Tala. Lamia's at home. She was tired.'

'I'm sick,' she managed weakly, but she could not even be sure that he had heard her before the door slammed after him. She listened. His quick steps rang out like wind chimes on the marble floors outside. Reluctantly, Zina rose from the bed and combed her hair. Her feet dragged through the mushy thickness of the white bedroom carpet. She looked down. That carpet was probably not helping her blocked nose and itching throat. Hadn't her mother ever heard of dust mites? The two inch high shag pile was probably teeming with enough creatures to populate a small country. Zina scratched her arms and tried to relax. It was less than a week until the wedding, and then she could get out of here and back to the wood-covered floors and clean white walls of her New York apartment. She climbed back into bed and lay there, her breathing shallow as she tried not to think about the years' worth of dust and dead skin cells that were hiding in the sinister cradle of her pillow.

As she had hoped would happen, Lamia found her husband responding with intent interest to the small item of conversation she had quietly introduced as they sat at their own dinner table that evening. He had a tendency to prefer bad news over good, and when it came to talking to him she had learned to sift the events and conversations of her day accordingly. When faced with negative reports, he could indulge his appetite for delicate criticism of the parties involved which was satisfying to him and soothing to her. And in fact, Lamia had begun to require daily this reassuring reminder that she was better off than most others, that people around her were unhappy for reasons that Kareem could so easily and eloquently articulate. Listening to him speak, she felt certain that the taint of such problems could not touch them, and the idea dripped scant, small droplets of warmth into the cold, dark hollow of her chest.

'Tala told you this herself?' Kareem looked at his wife, gauging.

She nodded but could not glance up for she was so close to teasing out the last chips of feta cheese from her salad. The cheese was crumbly and creamy, and fragments of it stuck to everything, tainting the cucumber and even the lettuce with fatty residues. She felt sickened at the sight of the tiny white curds, bright and taunting against the fresh green of the leaves. Irritated, she pushed her plate away from her.

'She told you she's having doubts?' Kareem persisted. He frowned at his wife's plate. Once again she had left the mound of salad mostly untouched. He would have to tell the cook to make a smaller one each day.

'Of course,' Lamia replied tersely. 'It wouldn't be a proper engagement for her without doubts.'

Kareem ignored the sarcasm. He felt a twitch of possibility, an itch in his groin, and he wanted to find out if there was substance to this situation. For Kareem did not care for Tala's fiancé. He was a loose cannon, a mould breaker, the kind of personality that could deteriorate quickly into an anarchist. And he was helping to run the country!

'What doubts?' Kareem asked. 'There's nothing wrong with him.'

Except that he's an anarchist, he thought, and worse, about to become a son-in-law to Omar and Reema. About to step up to the same footing that Kareem had spent the past few years enjoying alone. Kareem had earned a certain trust, a certain familial bond with his parents-in-law that he did not relish sharing with anyone else, especially someone like Hani, who sometimes had trouble understanding the subtle hierarchies of families and communities.

'I know there's nothing wrong with him,' said Lamia. She herself found Hani extremely handsome and very courteous. His manners were underlaid with real consideration; there was the assurance of depth beneath the surface and she found it inexplicably attractive. 'But she's not sure she feels passionately about him.'

Kareem snorted. 'Sometimes I forget she's older than you,' he said to Lamia. 'She's like a teenager. Passion!'

Lamia touched her forehead. She felt the stirrings of a headache between her eyebrows.

'It's not bad to want passion,' she said, trying to keep the tone of accusation out of her voice, and succeeding only modestly. She felt a pulse of apprehension at his potential response and was already preparing her defence (her head was pounding, she felt ill, she was only talking about Tala...) but luckily, he had not appeared to notice. His gleaming eyes were thinking, focused on his plate as he placed forkful after forkful of fragrant food into his mouth. Lamia felt dizzy with hunger, but the idea of the slaughtered lamb and cloying rice concoction sliding down into her stomach was too disgusting to contemplate.

Kareem finished his meal and Lamia waited while he reached for a piece of flatbread. She watched, her mouth slightly slack with tiredness, although she could not fathom what she had done all day to create such exhaustion within herself. As usual, he broke off a large piece of bread and then wiped his plate clean. First the right hand side, then the left, with a final sweep down his favourite part, the lamb juices in the middle. With an air of satisfaction he then placed the moistened bread into his mouth and sat back to chew. He felt tensely invigorated. He looked at his wife.

'What shall we do tonight?'

She swallowed. Might she ask? She essayed a smile, a quiet smile laden with promise. 'What about if we just go to bed early?'

It was the response he would have wished for, had he been capable of articulating to himself that he had sexual impulses at all. His occasional carnal urges inspired within his own mind a curdled mixture of desire and disgust; for at the moment of ultimate sexual release he felt completely lost and uncontrolled. It horrified Kareem that the world might begin to crash down around him and he would be powerless to do anything but make a final, groaning thrust towards the fulfillment of his own, gross animal instincts.

'You're going to shower first?' he said, and she nodded. She had showered but two hours ago, after her session at the gym, but if she was to receive any hope of satisfaction herself, she would need to clean herself again. She stood up from the table, which was already being cleared by their housekeeper and walked into the bathroom to undress.

Much worse for Tala than the daily battles with her mother over clothes, accessories and other wedding-related paraphernalia was the insomnia. Once again, in the weak, early hours of the morning, she awoke, hot and angry, as though snatched from a nightmare, although she could remember no immediate dream. She lay still within the warmed cotton sheets of her bed, keeping her breathing even and calm, trying to reduce herself back to that rare, soothing, restoring level of drowsiness. It was no use. Her mind brushed off the tricks she tried, and she opened her eyes and watched the weak light of dawn cast its slow illumination into her huge bedroom. The lazy luminosity of the sun on the ancient wall-hangings, on the carved bookshelves, on the softly-veined marble of the fireplace, calmed her. It was in these fragile moments of solitude that she succumbed to thoughts of Leyla. More than anything else, Tala held onto the memory of the night in Oxford, of the gentle fall into slumber when she had felt Leyla's arms about her. She could still recall the essence of that high emotion, of that exhausted happiness, and the knowledge that such an ecstatic feeling had to be so fleeting brought the sting of tears to her eyes.

At times like this, it was inconceivable to her that she should be even contemplating marriage to Hani. And yet it was inconceivable that she should consider building a life with Leyla, or with any woman. What lay between the two possibilities was a grey swamp in which she had been floating for all of her adult life, into which she had fled after each broken engagement, and from which she felt unaccountably sorry to have been rescued by each new fiancé. She was dimly aware that the events of her everyday life – work, friends, travel, the confidence with which she met the world – successfully covered the unpalatable fact of her inner, emotional flailing.

She turned over and stared at the gold travel clock her parents had given her for her last engagement. It was still only six thirty. She was sure that her father would be awake, sitting alone in the vast salon downstairs, drinking the thick, brackish coffee he loved, watching the business news on the oversized television, speeding through the newspapers; but she felt unequal to making conversation with him. She wanted to think out this problem further, to test the ground over which she was so reluctant to tread. Her head felt thick with weariness, but she forced herself to consider her situation. People, girls especially, often went through phases. At her boarding school, several girls in her class (herself included) developed passing crushes on one teacher or another, and one or two of those teachers had even favoured certain girls; a constant frisson, a shivering undertone of desire that made her believe that such excitement must be a natural part of female interaction.

But to be definitely, irretrievably homosexual would be extremely inconvenient. Back at university, in the grasp of that first, heady passion, she had gone as far as to imagine sharing her possible sexuality with her mother and father. In these imaginings, she was never back home in Amman; instead her parents would be visiting her, and at a louche coffee house somewhere near her university campus she would sit with them, relaxed, confident, burning with righteous determination. And she would begin the conversation:

'Remember you always said you wanted us to be happy?'

And then the dream would pause, for she could not actually recall them having said such a thing. Happiness was a concept that seemed to have passed her parents by. It was certainly not deemed a good enough reason to enter into the important transactions of life – such as work or marriage. She believed differently, or so she liked to think. But if she was not sure she would be happy with Hani, what was she doing marrying him?

Quickly, she rose from the rumpled sheets and walked across to her bathroom, turning on the shower while she brushed her teeth and undressed. The ready jets of hot water created damp wisps of soft vapour that rose about her head. She watched her reflection in the mirror. The breaths of steam were already touching the sparkling glass surface, slowly making opaque the area around her face until the white translucence of it obscured her features entirely.

Zina awoke sniffing, anxious to discover whether her symptoms had retreated. Since early childhood she had been cursed by a hyper awareness of herself and others, which had left her sensitive and nervous for much of her life, particularly since she had decided (at about the age of eleven) that her mother had no real or abiding interest in her wellbeing. She had taken this maternal apathy personally at first, until her early teenage years brought the revelation that her mother's attitude extended to each of her daughters equally, after which Zina felt not only rejected herself, but outraged on behalf of her sisters. Unequal to discussing any of this with Reema, Zina had instead rattled quietly between tense irritation and quiet despair with occasional excursions into moral outrage for anything that caught her attention as unjust. She began a regime of demonstrations, small and varied, during her early teens. At boarding school she resolutely refused to eat chicken because it came from battery farms, while on holidays back home in Amman, she spent long periods in the industrial-sized basement kitchen, explaining the concept of trade unions to Reema's army of bewildered Indian staff. By the time she cornered the halal butcher, after one of his deliveries of fresh carcasses to the house, in order to convince him that his methods of slaughter were inhumane, Reema had been forced to decide that her youngest child could not be allowed to remain in Amman until she had learned some decency and respect. After that, Zina spent the bulk of her school holidays with Tala or Lamia in America or London before she moved to New York to do her degree, and to think over, in freedom, the lasting effects on her psyche of the mortal pierce of her mother's rejection.

And now, she lay in bed heavily, lacking the will to get up. More disturbingly, she realised that this sapping of her inner strength had been going on for some time, and therefore could not conveniently be blamed on Amman, or her family, or the old friends she had been meeting here and who struck her now as so entirely alien. Maybe she was depressed. Depression was an illness, at least in the States, although here it was just deemed to be bad manners. She could not reconcile herself, however, to the idea that depression-as-an-illness might require drugs, and worse, therapy. Her family would never countenance it; they would categorise her as a psychotic loose cannon, which would be manifestly unfair and rather ironic, since this was how she had been forced to categorise half of them over the years.

She hauled herself into the bathroom as she considered all this, and then slung on a robe. She had to get out of this room and downstairs. She had to see Tala properly. God knows, it was almost impossible to talk to her alone, when the house was always filled with some person or another dropping by to offer congratulations or gossip.

It felt like a wonderful stroke of fate, then, when Zina stepped down from the last step and into the high-ceilinged living room to find

Tala alone, ensconced on the sofa. Abu Ali was bringing her tea. He had been with their family for thirty years, and during this time, they had heard news of seven children and fifteen grandchildren. Abu Ali had proudly arranged the marriages of every one of those children, not infrequently to their own first cousins, 'to keep what belongs to the family in the family,' he would stress. Zina wondered if Abu Ali had ever considered the disparity between the upbringing of his own daughters and the way in which she and her sisters had been raised. His sons worked fifteen hour days and his daughters were all at home with their small children, cooking, cleaning, often pregnant, absorbed in the challenge of scraping a life from the meagre incomes their husbands brought in.

She sank into the cream leather of the imposing sofa and leaned across to meet Tala's hug and kiss. Ironically, it was her sister who actually looked sick, Zina thought. Perhaps it was just exhaustion and the nervous tension that was a natural consequence of being trapped in the same house (however large) with Reema for three weeks; and even worse, only a few days before a wedding. There was a strong element of mental torture about it. The endless dinner parties at which the prospective bride was paraded like a prize heifer. The regular, inspirational words of advice on pleasing men that Reema felt it her duty to put out. Zina felt a pall of moroseness settle onto her.

'Is life really so bad?' Tala asked, smiling.

Zina shook herself and turned to return the smile, for the sentence was nothing more than a greeting, but she found herself weeping uncontrollably and inexplicably. And then she was aware of nothing except the comforting, childhood smell of the sofa, and the warmth of Tala's arm and chest against which she found herself pulled. Tala's low voice muttered something to Abu Ali, and she felt the old man move away. Within a few minutes Zina's sobbing had relaxed and softened to slow, silent tears, but she remained where she was, with her legs and back awkwardly twisted, because the pure consolation of her sister's arms was too hard to give up. Tala said nothing, just held her youngest sister to her, and waited.

To Tala there seemed to be something fitting and almost inevitable, about Zina's breakdown. The emotional outpouring seemed to suggest everything that was occurring in her own heart, it seemed reflective of the taut, delicate wires of stress that they all felt strung up inside their chests. And weddings, Tala thought, are supposed to be happy affairs. She felt a pointed prick of guilt. The happiness was supposed to start with the bride and groom and emanate out to everyone else. She kissed the top of Zina's head. Was Zina, who lay weeping in her arms, a reflection of her own misery? Had she somehow infected her sister with her own confusion and despair?

'What is it, *habibti*?' Tala asked quietly. She repeated the question at occasional intervals, while Zina cried quietly. She did not expect an answer yet, but instead used the words as a kind of soothing mantra, a reassuring reminder to Zina that she was there and that she cared.

Abruptly, Zina shifted and sat up, wiping the hot tears from her cheeks with her hands until she saw the box of tissues that Abu Ali had discreetly slipped within her reach. Tala leaned forward and touched her hand.

'What's the matter, *habibti*? Please tell me.'

Zina swallowed and blinked away the remnants of salty moisture from her aching eyes. 'David broke up with me,' she said. She frowned. It was not what she had planned to say, not right at this moment, nor did the sentence come close to expressing all the reasons for her current anxiety and sorrow. But it had spilled from her under the kind weight of Tala's eyes, and so Zina imagined the recent split from her boyfriend must have a deeper meaning than she herself had attributed it.

'Is he mad?' Tala said, and Zina had to smile at her sister's indignation, so genuinely grand in scale, despite the fact that she had never met David. 'Why?!'

'Because he's Jewish. And I'm Palestinian.'

Zina watched as Tala sat back and frowned for a moment, though her mouth had a suspiciously smile-like pucker at the edges.

'Jewish?'

'Yes. What's so funny?'

'Just picturing Mama and Baba's faces if it had worked out.'

But Zina could only sigh as more tears welled up.

'He can't imagine being married to a non-Jew,' she sniffed.

'You mean, he won't imagine it,' Tala returned, but Zina shook her head vehemently.

'His Jewish culture is a huge part of his identity. He's being open about not wanting to give it up.'

'Were you asking him to?'

Zina shook her head. 'But he wants Jewish kids and Hannakah and Passover..it would be impossible.'

'Then why on earth did he even bother going out with you? What kind of person gets emotionally entangled in a relationship, and even worse, lets you fall in love with him, when he feels there's no way forward?'

'Don't you ever make mistakes?' Zina asked, desperately. 'Sometimes you don't stop and rationalise everything so perfectly. Don't you ever just do something, even when you know deep down it's going to cause a problem?'

Zina felt unaccountably guilty, because she sensed a shift in her sister as she finished this last comment, felt a sudden discomfort emanating from Tala's side of the sofa, and all this from a moment's exasperation about her own mistakes with David. She was at a loss as to what she had said that could have bothered Tala so much, and her repeated questioning of her older sister yielded nothing except a tired smile and Tala's insistence that she was fine. By the time Zina looked up to see Kareem walking in, she had decided that she would give Tala some time and try to talk to her again later. In the meantime, the arrival of her brother-in-law, suavely impeccable in a suit and immaculate white shirt, only irritated her.

'No two women should look this amazing at seven in the morning,' he said, grinning.

His opening compliment appeared to have not even the slightest effect on either sister.

'You're up early, Kareem,' Tala said.

'I wanted to stop by and say hello to your father before I go to the airport,' Kareem paused to give their anticipation a moment to build. 'Sami's coming in from New York for the wedding.'

'I haven't seen your brother in years,' Zina said, conversationally. 'Does he still like musicals?'

Zina felt the hard prod of Tala's foot on her own, but when she looked at her sister, who appeared intently focused on the newspaper now, she saw again the hint of amusement in her mouth.

'I don't know,' Kareem said curtly, adjusting his watch. 'But I'm sure he's looking forward to seeing you, Zina.'

'Why?'

God, she was irritating. But luckily, Kareem noticed, she also seemed to be leaving.

'Will you excuse me? I have to get dressed,' Zina said, with barely a glance at him. He nodded, politely, and waited for her to leave before sitting down, keeping the creases in his trousers correct. He smiled at Tala, noting that she looked exhausted and nervous.

'How's Lamia?' Tala asked him.

'Lamia's in bed. She likes to take her time in the mornings.' With a delicate gesture to Abu Ali, Kareem signaled that he would like some coffee.

There were many more avenues of conversation open to her with her brother-in-law – his work, his family, his views on almost anything – but all of them spoke to her of a tedium she could not bear this morning and so she smiled and looked to the end of the cavernous room, where the wall was made up of two storey high sheets of glass that looked onto the gardens, the fruit groves and the hills beyond. The sun stroked the tops of the trees, and they could hear birds conferring, breaking the still silence of the morning.

'It's beautiful, isn't it?' Kareem had followed her gaze and was carefully attempting to establish a common interest, a connection between them that he now realised was generally lacking. She had never appeared to like him much, he felt, although it was hard to state such a fact definitively. After all, they attended the same family dinners, and laughed and joked together, but they existed in the same space rather than actively forming a relationship. This had never concerned Kareem before now, but he realised that if he hoped to achieve the status of confidante to Tala, he would have to make her feel trusting and warm towards him. It was one of those requirements that women had.

'It's lovely,' she agreed, her eyes fixed on the view. She stifled a yawn. 'I'm not sleeping any more,' she said.

Now this unsolicited confession was good fortune indeed, he thought. 'Really?' he said. He sat forward on the deep leather couch, a look of genuine concern etched into his handsome features. 'Why?'

The refreshments arrived at this moment, giving Kareem time to think of a follow-up question if this one should be met with muteness. Tala sprinkled a small spoon of sugar into her glass of mint tea and stirred it. The sweet, vegetal scent of the liquid was comforting to her. She looked at Kareem.

'I guess pre-wedding jitters and all that.'

'Anything serious?'

To give the suggestion that the question was simply throwaway, Kareem did not wait for an answer, but brought his own tiny cup of Arabic coffee delicately to his lips, successfully avoiding his thin moustache.

Tala smiled wanly. 'No.'

'Good.' He sat back again, as if satisfied. 'Because this is not a step to take lightly. This is the rest of your life. You have to be sure of what you're doing.'

She was surprised. She would not have expected him, of all people, to stress the importance of certainty over form. On an impulse she turned to him.

'Tell me something,' she said. 'Were you absolutely sure when you married my sister?'

He grinned roguishly. 'I had to be, or she would have killed me.' Once again, the attempted charm fell flat, the lightness of touch was too heavy. She sketched a half smile in acknowledgment but then sat watching him with ethereal, dark eyes that unsettled him.

'Of course I was sure,' he said, matching her serious look. 'I had not one doubt that this was the girl I wanted to be with.'

'Why?'

He raised his eyebrows. 'Because I loved her so much. Because our characters were suited, our values. All the important things.' He leaned in to her slightly, and his voice dropped. 'I think if I had felt even a slight doubt, I would not have done it.'

Their eyes met and stayed locked together for a moment. She could see within them only honest concern and kindness; a decency she had not previously credited him with. She blinked, and spoke quickly:

'What if the doubt is misleading? What if you couldn't find a rational reason for that doubt?' It felt strange to be so open with Kareem of all people, but her nerves were at breaking point; she was desperate for advice, and Zina was so much in the depths of her own misery that it had not felt right to bother her.

'Are doubts supposed to be rational? Is love?' he replied with a sage smile. 'I think you need to trust your instincts, Tala. I'm all for rationality, but there are times when you know in your heart – in your gut – what to do. Even if you can't justify it in your head.'

Tala was shocked and now regarded him with suspicion. 'You're telling me to break it off?'

'No!' he said, alarmed at his aim being so clearly articulated.

'Yes, you are.'

'You're telling me you have doubts...' He cut himself off, nipping his petulance in the bud and laced his hands together, giving the impression of deep thought. 'It's not wrong to go against the grain, Tala. If you marry Hani, I'll be the first one dancing at your wedding. But if you don't, I'll support you every step of the way.'

Abruptly, Kareem stood up. 'Anyway, I should be going. I don't want to keep my brother waiting.' He paused to look into her eyes once more with a nod of understanding. 'If ever you want to talk about anything, I'm here. Okay?'

Tala nodded, hesitantly, and tried to appear grateful, but she was too caught up in her own racing thoughts to pay attention to form. She heard the ringing tones of Kareem's steps walking briskly out and through the hallway to the front door.

Tala looked away, out of the windows, at the garden. Her own family, except perhaps Zina, were evidently aware of her doubts – she had spoken quite openly to Lamia about them – but not one of them had stepped forward to talk to her seriously, to offer support or advice, except for her brother-in-law, and his concern was so uncharacteristic that Tala was certain he must have some ulterior motive. She felt alone, marooned in the centre of a seamless stream of parties and dinners. People were whirling past – people whom she had known for all or most of her life and who apparently cared about her – and they laughed and talked and argued about politics and ate and shopped and congratulated; but not one had paused and looked into her eyes. She wanted a lifeline, the reassurance that someone, somewhere understood her, but there was none to be found. Again, she thought of Leyla, and the focus, however fleeting, awakened a yearning within Tala. Leyla would understand, of course, but Tala could hardly picture her features any more; the girl already seemed to belong to some past life; in fact, she might have been nothing more than a dream, an enveloping, pleasurable, warming dream that had passed too quickly and left Tala gasping in the icy reality of wakefulness.

Chapter 10

IT WAS THE THIRD TIME that Maya had called up the stairs the alert that breakfast would be ready imminently, and still there was no response from any of them. Leaving the eggs spitting in the pan she stomped up the first five steps to listen. Her husband was in the shower, of course, having waited for her first call to actually tear himself away from the business news and clean up. Yasmin had showered half an hour ago, but all that emanated from her room was loud music; and Leyla..who knew any more, what was going on with Leyla? Something had changed her since she had stopped working with her father in order to finish editing her novel. Although she was pleased Leyla had found a publisher, Maya had expected that to be the end of the writing for a while. All that sitting in front of computers fretting about words could not be good for a person, Maya felt, and although being proved right was always a comfort, her vindication was tempered by fear - for Leyla was proving a handful now, unhappy and angry all the time, and frankly, Maya felt too old and tired to be dealing with an overgrown adolescent.

The eggs were overcooked by the time she descended and crossed the wide kitchen to place her hand on the frying pan handle once more. She looked at their wilted brown lacy edges and the rubber solidity of the yolks with dismay. Throwing them out was not an option. Maya had grown up starved for eggs, eating her breakfast at a lop-sided wooden table in India surrounded by too many brothers and sisters and a father who kept faultless account of the paltry, weekly allocation of six eggs that lay in their box on a shelf far above the stove. Even now, the sight of a soft, fresh yolk breaking across her plate stirred up suppressed desire within her and also a species of panic – that the oozing, liquid gold would be thinned to non-existence unless she could quickly round up the spreading edges with her bread and lift the captured yolk to her mouth.

Sam was downstairs already, the master of the two minute shower, and to Maya's satisfaction, Leyla followed behind him. She looked tired, even though she went to bed early and was sleeping half the day as well. She was wrapped in a thin dressing gown, her feet bare on the cold kitchen tiles.

'You'll catch a cold. Where are your slippers?' Maya asked.

'Is there any juice?' Leyla asked.

'Yes,' said Yasmin, breezing in. 'If you like an old vintage.'

Leyla grinned at her sister, whose hair was wet from the shower. The freshness of her scent cut through the spice-laden atmosphere of the kitchen.

'I'll go get some fresh juice,' Yasmin said. 'I need a proper coffee anyway.'

'Not with wet hair. You'll catch pneumonia,' Maya counselled.

'You catch pneumonia from a germ, Mum, not from wet hair.'

'Of course, you're the doctor. Go then but if you're lying in hospital tomorrow, don't expect me to visit you.'

Maya sniffed and turned to the stove where she teased the eggs out of the pan as though they might escape if she removed the threat of the spatula.

'I'll visit you,' Leyla said, deadpan, as Yasmin disappeared to the shops. She flicked on the kettle and peered into the waiting teapot which was big enough for five people but which held only one bag. As usual, she thought savagely, her mother was intent on making everyone suffer the sipping of a weak, coloured solution for breakfast, while they sat in a forty thousand pound kitchen in a two million pound home, in order to save the cost of the extra teabags. She reached up and added more tea to the pot, then poured over the boiling water. She could feel Maya watching her from the corner of her eye, could sense the stiffening of her mother's body at the perceived waste, and Leyla turned and regarded her with directness, daring her to make an issue out of a spoonful of cheap tea dust in a cheap bag.

Nothing was said, and Leyla made it back to the table without reproach. She sat down and looked at her cold, stiff egg. It looked exactly like a toy egg, made of flexible rubber, and out of curiosity, she leaned forward to smell it, but only her father's sudden scent, diffusing across the round table, touched her nostrils. It was fresh and soapy, mixed with the ozone fragrance of his aftershave, and the grasping touch of his just-applied hairspray which caught you in the throat like a dry poison before suddenly letting go. It was the smell of morning, the smell she had grown up with, that had been her breakfast companion for so many thousands of days, and she was suddenly grateful for it, and the gratitude made her throat catch and her eyes fill with tears. She swallowed and tried to cover her emotion – these newly naked, uncontrolled feelings were embarrassing and ridiculous. She seemed to walk around all day on the point of tears – the lightest, most unexpected sensory touch could arouse her to crying.

Sam looked up as he ate, and noticed his daughter's watery eyes. The stress that the sight induced compelled him to finish the rest of his breakfast in two large bites. This had the dual effect of comforting him, while giving her time to recover, after which he was able to ask her if she was all right.

'I'm fine,' she said. She waited a beat, drawing on the well of bitterness within to aid her recovery. 'It's just the sight of this egg. I don't like to see anything that's suffered this much…'

Maya sighed audibly, and Leyla felt a fleeting shame, that she had swapped her unidentifiable sorrow for pointless and hurtful sarcasm. But it was too late. The comment was made, and she had at least regained control of herself.

'Don't have it if you don't want it,' said Maya manfully. 'I'll just throw it out to the birds.'

'How can you give a bird an egg?' Leyla asked quietly. It smacked of weirdness, of a kind of pre-cannibalism. 'Birds lay eggs. They shouldn't eat them.'

'So now you are a bird expert,' Maya said.

'Ornithologist,' Leyla muttered with quiet malevolence.

Sam was standing now, putting on his tie (he habitually brought it downstairs with him but only wore it after the danger of spilling his breakfast was over) and he shot his daughter a stern, warning look. This had the effect of making Leyla feel small and guilty at the same time, and without meaning to, she burst into tears.

Maya was intently dipping the point of her toast into her powdery, dried up yolk as if constant stabbing might somehow soften the unyielding egg, but even she had to look up at this. Sam was behind Leyla's chair in a moment, placing his large, firm hands on the sides of her arms. She could feel his head turn, could sense the concerned, helpless glance that was passing between her parents.

'What is it?' he asked quietly. She took a breath that manifested itself as a hiccupped sob and then stopped crying. She looked down at her lap, at the thin material that covered her thinning legs. She was eating but losing weight. She had a publisher for her book, but took little joy in it. She was crying but knew she ought to be happy.

'I don't know,' she whispered. It was a true statement, for she had not yet managed to admit that what was troubling her, that a ridiculous yearning for a girl she had spent only a few days with, was worth this kind of pain.

'Do you want to see the doctor?' Sam asked.

It was a clumsy attempt, but at least it was an attempt and she was grateful for it. She turned and smiled briefly, to reassure him, and he was relieved by this and quickly stepped away, a movement towards the door, the car, the secure, compact world of the office.

After two more days of watching his daughter exist within the house like a nervous, feverish spectre, Sam spoke at length over dinner one evening about how he felt he needed to hire more help at work. His conversation was directed ostensibly to his wife, although Leyla divined at once that it was aimed more particularly at her. Her father spoke in ringing, slightly over-enunciated tones, as though to ensure that every nuance of his unsubtle carrot was picked up, and Maya nodded and exclaimed in all the right places. The very idea of being once more imprisoned for nine hours a day in the beige-walled office, overlooking the tarred expanse of the car park turned Leyla's stomach. If she was depressed now, she would only become suicidal if she was made to sit at the brown desk each day, working out percentages, reconciling receipts, checking the wording of policy documents....

'It would only be temporary,' her father was saying. 'Until we find a new person to start.' He was looking directly at her now, Leyla noticed.

'What?' she asked, slackly.

'I need help,' he said. 'If you're not busy.'

'Busy?!' Maya began, a snort of scorn in her voice, but she subsided at once beneath the look that her husband shot her.

Leyla did not know how to refuse. He was kind, her father, and his eyes met hers with such invitation. He was trying to help her, she realised. He was offering her his hand in the only way he knew how, a hand to pull her out of the treacle pool of her own self-pity.

'Okay,' she said.

He grinned, and helped himself to another chapatti. 'Good. To-morrow, eight thirty. We'll go in together.'

A week of regular hours at work had not evolved into the hellish entrapment that Leyla had imagined it would. Time flew by in the early mornings, time spent completing the series of actions necessary to ensure that she arrived at her desk at half past eight each day. She was aware of the sharp, taut touch of the shower on her head, the hot water pouring away in rivulets down her body. She tasted the crisp, rushed toast, the warm softness of too much butter on her tongue. There was the need to dress, to find proper clothes to wear and real shoes to replace the slippers with which she had shuffled through the house while writing. And then the car journey, the radio news of a world far beyond this one of hers, which was bound by closer horizons.

Arriving at work, she was surprised to find so much paper on her desk. It was the same work as always – the opportunities for inspiration were always bound to be limited – but the sheer volume of it caught her off guard, and she began to hold a private competition with herself each day, to see how far she could get.

And there were people at the office. Women who had worked for her father for years. There was talk and laughter and self-deprecating complaints and the quick fire touch of sarcasm on everything they said, and she had to match their tone or be lost in her own sealed world forever. And she found it difficult to smile at a joke or make an ironic comment and still nurture the depression that lingered within. It was hard to remember her dissatisfaction when she was caught between meetings, phone calls and emails and what eventually emerged from her remaining lack of enthusiasm for her work was not unmitigated misery but a new inspiration for writing. As had happened so long before, ideas and words and unrequited feelings began to filter through the tracts of her mind that were not occupied with her daily tasks, like coffee dripping through a perco-lator. When she got home at night, she would spread out her paper and pens on the dining room table and write down the dribbling words, and as quickly as she caught those drops, more would come, until there was a trickle of sentences that she dammed to form the continuation of a new story. The slow pleasure and small pulses of intense excitement she felt at these times seemed very much like happiness. And while a small part of her was embarrassed that her apparent depression could have been brushed off so quickly, like crumbs from a dense, stale cake, she was sufficiently relieved that she worked hard not to look down and slip back into those depths again.

Chapter 11

A T TEN O'CLOCK in the morning, Reema descended her magnificent hanging staircase with a blinding headache, which she was quite certain could be attributed to the injection of Botox into the last, feathered line on her forehead that she had insisted on the day before. With extreme irritation, she noted that the line was still there when she squinted into the depths of her antique bedroom mirror. She felt tense and tired and managed only a poor shuffle into the dining room, where her peripheral vision caught sight of Tala and Lamia seated for breakfast, before her eyes settled on a mirage of steaming coffee and a cigarette that lay shimmering on the table before her winged chair. When she sat down and found that, in fact, neither caffeine nor nicotine were ready for instant inhalation she sent up an ululating scream of protest to the hapless maid who stood hovering behind her. Within moments, the coffee was produced, and a freshly lit cigarette placed between her ring-encrusted fingers. She drew in long and hard, taking from the kick of dense, tarry fumes the same satisfaction as a diver coming up for air. Only then, as the smoke around her head cleared, and with the scalding, thick coffee raised to her lips, did she glance up and see that Omar and Kareem were also at the table with her. Rather more alarmingly, there was another man with them and as she took him in, as her brain began its slow, creaking shift into consciousness, she regretted her recent guttural howl to the staff, and her defeated trudge into the room. When there were guests, she made a point of sweeping into rooms. She produced a charming smile in an attempt to reduce the impact of her substandard entrance, but only when Kareem introduced his brother formally did she recognise Sami. She had not seen him for several years, and reminded him of this fact at once.

'I live in New York, Aunty,' Sami told her.

'Like Zina,' she replied. 'You don't see her there?'

'It's a big place. The whole population of Jordan would get lost just in Manhattan.'

Kareem smiled, faintly embarrassed.

'He just moved there, Aunty,' Kareem explained quickly. But his mother-in-law was right, over a period of two months in New York, Sami should have at least begun to make an effort to see Zina. He had not given it enough consideration since Sami had moved there, but it did not reflect well on his family that his brother was not looking out for Omar's youngest daughter in the big city they both shared. Kareem considered, while he carefully straightened the line of his cutlery. In fact, if Sami and Zina got to know each other, they might even…

'Have you met Zina?' Reema asked. 'She's very beautiful, you know. And she cooks.'

Kareem beamed. There were times he felt that he and Reema were of one mind. It was such a useful faculty to have, this concordance, this happy harmony with his in-laws. Sami shifted in his seat and smiled politely.

'She's too beautiful for me, Aunty.'

That was a bizarre reply, Reema thought. How could anyone (least of all Zina) be too beautiful for any man? What did he mean by such an answer? Was he trying to be sophisticated? Perhaps this kind of phrase passed for wit in America. She studied Sami as he self-consciously took a sip of his mint tea. He was handsome, though perhaps not as clean cut as Kareem; he wore his hair slightly longer and his clothes were more fashionable, more black, more New York. Which was not necessarily a bad thing, since Zina always dressed as though she was expecting an invitation to a funeral. Two daughters married to two brothers. She had been so focused on getting Tala married over the past few years that she had neglected to properly maneuver on behalf of her youngest child. Sami would be a coup – for Kareem's family even more so, she quickly reminded herself, since they were not in the same league financially or socially as she and Omar. But then so few people were. And it would remove from her shoulders the burden of worry about her wayward, over-sensitive younger daughter. A gentle click within Reema's mind placed a sepia-edged picture there, of Lamia and Kareem, Tala and Hani, Zina and Sami. The pleasure of that vision coincided with the gratifying pulse of nicotine that was coursing through her now, at last, as she embarked on her second cigarette. It was a golden moment of the mind but Reema could not pause to enjoy it. There was clearly some arranging to be done.

In a voice that was deeply commanding, Kareem was expounding (again) his own solution for the crisis between Palestine and Israel. Tala had noticed that as soon as Hani had arrived to join them for breakfast, Kareem felt compelled to move the discussion to politics.

She shifted further back in her chair – a plush red velvet construction – and toyed with the food on her plate, a snowy mound of labaneh yoghurt, sliced cucumbers, green olives and dried thyme. It was her favourite, traditional breakfast, but she could do no more than try the cucumber this morning.

As the talk continued, Tala closed her eyes for a moment and felt only the softness of light-tinged shade. The sweetness of the sensation was intoxicating. Gone was the furniture-stuffed room; gone was Lamia's disinterested, polite face; removed were Kareem's insistent eyes, and her father's tapping fingers. It was peace, she felt, to sit there with sight blocked out. She felt a wave of sleep lap up to her, caressing her with the sweet stroke of its promise of release and renewal. She was deeply tired; had been exhausted since her mother's visit to London had turned into a relentless trawling around dress shops, restaurants and bespoke home furnishing establishments, all in final readiness for the wedding. The forced absorption with every, minute, ridiculous detail of her nuptials had acted like a soporific to numb her true feelings, and at the time, haunted by her last walk away from Leyla, Tala had been grateful for it.

'Are you okay?' Hani's soft voice was gentle to her ears and she opened her eyes and smiled at him. She nodded and he touched her hand for a moment. There was reassurance in the touch, a certain safety, and it brought to the fore her affection for him. It was for Hani's sake, for the sake of their future together, that she had not attempted to pursue Leyla by phone or letter and when her resolve had been weak, the busy stress of the wedding preparations and her mother's close proximity had been enough to ensure the communication between them would remain closed forever. Tala swallowed a soft sigh and looked at Hani. His attention had turned back to Kareem.

'Palestinians have no other weapons,' Kareem was saying. 'If we are driven to use ourselves, to suicide missions, then that's part of guerrilla warfare.'

That she had to open her eyes and ears to the old record of Kareem's views, which almost always echoed the views of the majority (he would never dare to think on his own, let alone stand by an original thought, even if one should miraculously occur to him) seemed too hard to Tala just now. Her mind felt raw, like a field of open wounds; her senses were offended by anything around her that was ugly, and at this moment it seemed that everything that touched her eyes and ears was unsightly. She looked at her brother-in-law fiercely.

'It's barbaric,' she said. 'This idea of martyrdom, of paradise waiting for you if you kill yourself and take innocent people with you, is obscene. It's pure brainwashing, but no-one will admit it.' Her voice was rising, but she felt powerless to control it.

'They're not killing innocent people, mama,' said Reema, picking through the meaningless debris of her daughter's so-called argument to find the one aspect she could comment on. 'They're killing Israelis.'

'They're killing children,' said Hani firmly. The side of Reema's mouth that did not have a cigarette protruding from it twitched palpably at this insolence, but before she could respond, Kareem came to her defence.

'Children who will grow up to be Israeli soldiers,' replied Kareem, reaching to wipe from the glass-topped table a tiny smudge of water left by his wife's glass. 'With all due respect,' he continued, straightening the cutlery within his reach, 'You and I have never suffered like our Palestinian countrymen. You and I have never watched our tiny house, that we were forced into after Israeli guns drove us from our land, being demolished because they wanted to teach someone else in the village a lesson. You and I have never held a dying baby in our arms because an Israeli gun shot him in response to rock-throwing. You and I have never watched our children crying from hunger because we ran out of milk during a curfew.'

It was a stirring piece of rhetoric, but Tala was willing to wager that Kareem himself had never placed his perfectly polished shoes within miles of a refugee camp.

'If I remember rightly, you were busy the last time we went to a refugee camp to interview people for jobs,' she reminded him.

'I was busy holding the fort at the office, for your father, that day,' explained Kareem patiently. 'And Lamia and I went to the refugee charity dinner just last month.'

'Where the refugees washed the dishes,' muttered Sami, under his breath, but with just enough projection for Tala to hear. She caught his eye and smiled briefly.

'No-one is condoning Israel's actions.' Hani took over calmly.

Kareem leaned his solid form back in his chair and cast a quick, smiling glance at Omar; it was a smile of companionship, Tala noted irritably. A smile of condescension towards the opening of Hani's earnest argument that they would nevertheless hear out with avuncular patience, while waiting for the day when Hani matured to their higher level of understanding.

'But if we blindly condone everything that we do,' Hani continued, 'if we don't critique ourselves, we're not going to progress either. We have to be practical when it comes to Israel.'

'What you call being practical sounds to me like being defeatist,' interrupted Kareem, with a serious nod to Reema.

'Then you're not listening properly,' Hani replied. 'Do you know I wanted to be a violinist when I was young?'

'Did you?' Tala asked. An image came to her mind of a small, serious boy in a dinner jacket holding a burnished wooden instrument, a snapshot of hope.

Hani nodded. 'But here, and especially at that time, something so artistic, so unreliable, so impractical, especially for a boy, was unthinkable. If your father had a business, and you wanted to be a writer or an artist or a singer, then too bad - you joined the business. We live in a world where practicality is prized. And yet, in politics, where in fact the Palestinians have almost nothing to negotiate with, no-one wants to be practical.'

'Because we have honour,' Kareem proclaimed proudly. 'You've been a politician too long, Hani. I respect your views; but for myself, I have to aim high, otherwise how do dreams come true?'

He ended his carefully modulated statement with a nod to his parents-in-law. Omar cleared his throat, preparing to speak for the first time that morning.

'Hani has a point,' he said. 'We have to cut out emotion and look at it as a business deal.'

Kareem nodded respectfully at his father-in-law, switching horses with such practised ease that no-one even noticed him jump. 'When you put it that way, Ammo, it begins to make sense.'

Omar looked away, pleased, but slightly embarrassed under the clear, admiring gaze of his son-in-law. When he glanced up again, Kareem was reaching out a hand to Hani. They were good men, he thought, and his daughters were lucky to have them.

As dusk took hold of the room, and she switched on lamps, Zina thought she must have misheard.

'What?' she asked Lamia, staring at her in dismay. 'Did you say Sami?'

In spite of the freshly pressed lines of her silk dress, Tala lay back on Zina's bed and smiled sardonically. Zina looked at her, exasperated. It was fine for Tala to relax and enjoy the sheer stupidity of a moment like this, but dinner was due to be served in ten minutes, there were at least thirty people downstairs having cocktails, Zina could find nothing to wear and now Lamia was here making all sorts of crazy suggestions.

'He likes you a lot, you know.'

'Yeah, well, he seems nice,' returned Zina.

She pulled off the dress she had just tried on and flipped through the remaining clothes in her closet. Lamia watched, trying not to wring her hands.

'Then why is it so out of the question? He's very nice, very handsome, well educated.' She paused, listening to the irritating click of the wooden hangers. 'And he wears black. You would match perfectly,' she added, appraising Zina's wardrobe with distaste. Zina swung round and fixed her sister with a burning look.

'He's gay.'

Lamia sat down. The content of the statement was hardly a shock to her, but its audible utterance was. Tala sat up reluctantly, for the gentle cradling of the pillow had been infinitely soothing to the pressure in her temples. Beside her, Zina stood angrily over Lamia.

'He's not gay,' was Lamia's desperate reply.

'And the Pope isn't Catholic,' noted Zina.

Tala laughed despite herself. 'Being gay is not a crime, Lamia,' Tala said. 'Zina is just pointing out a fact.'

'It's not a fact.' Lamia's voice was rising higher, driven by the certainty that her sisters were intent on bringing down Kareem's wrath upon her.

'Please,' Tala laughed. 'Everyone knows he's gay. Even if they're scared to say it to your face,' she added pointedly.

Zina's muffled voice carried back to them from her walk-in closet where she was disentangling a black dress from a hanger. 'I bumped into him one time in the Village with his boyfriend.'

Lamia's eyes widened. 'Did he introduce him like that?'

'Of course not. But it was extremely clear.'

'It's not clear.' Lamia was pacing now, as if the desperate scuff of her heels on the carpet might erase the reality of her brother-in-law's sexuality. 'And if it is, it's a phase. Don't ever repeat this to anyone. It would jeopardise his chances of getting married. Kareem's trying to persuade Sami to come back to Amman to live. It would be a better influence on him.'

'Perfect,' Zina said. 'Then of course I'll marry him. I haven't been doing enough social welfare work. Maybe rehabilitating gays would be just the thing.'

'My God, Lamia,' Tala said quietly. 'Are you so scared of your husband that you're willing to sacrifice your own sister's happiness by setting her up with his gay brother?'

Zina turned and watched Lamia squirm.

'It's a phase..' Lamia squeaked.

'Homosexuality is not a phase,' Tala said. 'Do you really think Sami can just change?'

Lamia's blinking eyes were cast down to the carpet, but when she raised her head, they showed a flash of anger that Tala felt as a kick of misgiving in her stomach.

'I think you would know more about that than anyone else,' she hissed, and turned on her heel, slamming the door behind her.

Zina turned to Tala with narrowed eyes that spoke of her disgust at Lamia, and then she stood straighter and held out her arms, a silent query about the suitability of the dress she was now wearing. Tala nodded approval, although she had hardly noticed the garment.

'Let's go downstairs,' Tala suggested. She felt a sudden desire to move; her nerves crackled with energy, her limbs were restless for motion. All the disgust and disappointment she felt at Lamia's behaviour could be just as credibly directed at herself for deceiving Hani when she felt passionately about Leyla. She swallowed, a vain attempt to loosen the dryness of her constricted throat, and with a head that was now spinning, tried to focus on Zina, applying her make up. She got as far as watching the lipstick being chosen when she felt the room move suddenly from beneath her, and then plunge into blackness.

Chapter 12

WITH HER NEWFOUND PURPOSE and confidence, Leyla had recently become the object of attentions that she had not sought herself. Having been unable to find any sign of lesbian women around her for years, they now seemed to be everywhere. The previous week, in the coffee shop down the road from the office where she had stopped to pick up a drink, she was flirted with by the female barista. And not more than a few days later, she found it almost unfathomable when after a party at the home of some friends, a young woman whom she had spent almost an hour talking to about music, casually asked her if she'd like to go out the following week.

'Go out?' Leyla had asked, encompassing perhaps a little less eloquence than she would have hoped.

The girl nodded, blue eyes smiling. 'Like on a date,' the girl clarified. Leyla knew she had not contained her surprise enough because she saw alarm touch the features opposite her.

'Sorry, I thought you might be..I mean, I'm gay. I thought…'

Leyla tried to convey her nonchalance with a casual flicking back of her hair, but succeeded only in knocking over a candle that sat on the table behind her. Once the two of them had managed to stamp out a flaming paper napkin and had scraped up the hot wax, Leyla felt able to reply.

'No, that's fine,' she stuttered. And then, before her courage should fail, she added. 'I'd love to'

It was now the day before that date and Leyla had already forgotten exactly what she had talked about with the blue-eyed girl that had drawn her to accept the offer. Nevertheless, something about the certainty of the moment's attraction, the solidity of a date, whether anything came of it or not, had spurred her to have a talk with her parents. A serious talk. The kind of talk she had never had occasion to trouble them with yet in her life.

As she pulled into the driveway and got out of the car, Leyla felt nauseous. It was approaching eight in the evening, and between the time she had left the office ten minutes before, and the moment that she arrived at her home, the world had darkened. The pleasant nuances of the late summer twilight had dispersed, covered over by a bleaker, more ominously grey hue. She looked up at the house. It looked dark and deserted, a haunted mansion within whose cavernous walls only the parsimonious spirit of her mother flitted from bedroom to living room, conserving the electric lights. Her father was in London with a client. Yasmin was out of town for three days working on a catering job. Though Leyla would have preferred to speak to her sister first, the blind craving, the overwhelming need she had felt building all week would no longer be held back.

She pushed open the door, and spent a minute divesting herself of her coat, briefcase and umbrella. By the time she moved forward into the large hallway, she had run through ten different introductions to the subject on her mind and every muscle in her slim body was generally tuned to an unbearably fine pitch of tension. So when Maya leaped out at her from the shadowed staircase, uttering a primal yell and brandishing a poker, Leyla felt her heart flirting with a cardiac arrest. She staggered back against the wood-panelled wall, almost panting.

'Oh, it's you!' said Maya.

'Who the hell were you expecting? Jack the Ripper?' Leyla asked, unable to articulate more than a ragged whisper.

'Watch your language,' Maya countenanced. 'I heard someone sneaking around. I'm on my own here, you know. No-one else is going to protect me.'

Without further explanation she turned and went back to the living room, where she replaced the poker among the other useless fire-tending paraphernalia that rested by the gas-fed hearth, and sat down in front of the television.

'Mum, I need to talk to you,' Leyla began, but she was at a disadvantage, for she was now competing for airspace with a soap opera. Maya's eyes were fixed doggedly on the screen where a tired-looking older woman had just discovered that her drug-addicted daughter was pregnant. This cheered Maya immensely. It relieved her beyond expression to see before her the acute suffering of other people, even characters on a screen (because after all, these characters were based on real life) and to be able to favourably compare her own problems with theirs.

'Mum!'

Maya became aware of Leyla's insistent voice in the background. She sighed. At least her daughters were home with her, not running around having sex with strange men. She ought to be thankful, and in recognition of this newly felt gratitude, Maya heroically switched off the television in order to listen to her daughter.

The sudden silence, combined with Maya's expectant eyes upon her, startled Leyla and she found that she could not speak.

'I'm making some pasta,' Maya said, quickly leading the way to the kitchen, for there was something about the mutely pleading way her child was looking at her that was making her nervous.

'You're not sick are you?' Maya asked.

'No, I'm fine. Really good, in fact.' Leyla cleared her throat.

'Really happy, actually.' She coughed, for her voice felt seized and thick.

Maya's internal problem-detecting antennae shot up at this unusual response, and quivered tremulously, probing the air around her daughter. This triple, insistent reply, combined with Leyla's anxiety and phlegmy cough made her instantly alert. Briskly and with mild panic, she stirred at the boiling pasta, willing it to cook quickly.

'Ali called,' she said, over her shoulder. Just the mention of his name reassured Maya in some way and she smiled. 'He's a wonderful boy.'

Leyla took a short step into the kitchen. 'I'm not happy with him, Mum.'

'Then Aunty Gulshan's son is looking for someone,' suggested Maya, not without an air of desperation. 'He's very successful!'

'He's a bookie.'

'And tall and handsome,' persisted Maya.

'He's six foot seven,' replied Leyla. 'All I can see is his navel.'

'Well, then, you'll have tall children!'

'Mum, I can't be happy with him!' Leyla coughed again. 'The same way I'm not happy with Ali. And I've always known why, but I was hoping the reason I thought was the reason might not really be the reason, and that things might change, but they never have. And now I know for sure that what I've been feeling all these years is actually the right thing and there's nothing wrong with it....'

'Do you want cheese on this?' Maya asked, her head having momentarily disappeared in the burst of steam that issued as she desperately dumped the half-cooked spaghetti into a colander. Her voice was pitched at a level that suggested rapidly mounting hysteria, for even amongst the confused torrent of her daughter's rushing words, it was becoming all too clear to her that Leyla was about to confess something horrible, something Maya would rather not hear, ever.

'Mum, please listen, I'm just trying to say…'

'There's olive oil over there, if you want it.' Maya moved to the table, then changed her mind, picked up her plate and made for the relative safety of the living room, where the television stood only feet away, ready, just waiting to be turned on.

'Mum,' Leyla said, following her, confused but determined. 'I'm gay!'

If Maya had been able to scream and faint without feeling embarrassed, she would have done so but, as it was, she simply remained rooted to the spot, her plate of overly al dente pasta (free of cheese or oil) in one hand, and the television remote control in the other. In the hallway, the muffled sound of the front door slamming reached them both, followed by a cheery confirmation from Sam that he was home.

As her husband strode in, Maya became aware that she was standing like a statue, lips quivering in shock, armed only with the congealing spaghetti. She watched Sam's anxious gaze go from his wife to his daughter.

'What did I miss?' he asked.

Leyla looked at him, tears in her eyes. 'I'm gay,' she whispered.

Sam stared in disbelief. 'But I've only been gone two hours.'

He looked at Leyla's pale, uncertain face regarding him with forlorn hope, then looked down. This news was certainly a surprise to him, mainly because he had never taken a moment to consider his childrens' private lives, except when Maya regaled him with the virtues of one or other of their boyfriends and, even then, he paid minimal attention, since he could not really say that he much cared who either of them was with, as long as they were decent, and as long as he did not have to picture them sleeping with his daughter.

Leyla turned to her mother. 'You always said you just wanted us to be happy.'

'I lied,' Maya reassured her. She sniffed back the tears of anger she felt stinging her eyes.

'Don't cry, please, Mum,' Leyla said. Maya detected a note of regret in her daughter's voice. She cried.

'Who did this to you?' she demanded through her sobs.

'Mum, I haven't caught a disease. I'm just gay, like I have brown hair.'

When would she stop saying that word? Irate, Maya turned on her.

'First you stop coming to mosque, now you are up to your neck in sin!'

'It's not a sin.'

'It's a huge sin!'

'According to who?' Leyla was close to tears now.

'According to God!' Maya yelled.

'What kind of a God is that? I don't accept it!' Leyla yelled back.

'Then you will burn in hell,' stated Maya, her eyes piercing Leyla's with a righteous fury that gave her the courage to confront this appalling deviance and call it by its proper name.

'That's enough.' Sam's firm voice cut through the thick air and brought Maya to a stop. Incensed, she glared at him, paused to toss the plate of ruined pasta on the table and stormed upstairs.

Leyla looked down and stared at the rug. It was a swirling pattern that had flecks of beige and russet but which was primarily brown, a choice her mother had made because it would be easier to clean. She felt her father's arm around her, felt him holding out his capacious handkerchief which she took gratefully.

'If I could help it, I would,' Leyla said, blowing her nose. 'But I can't.'

'I know,' he replied. 'I know.'

When Tala shivered back into consciousness, she found herself lying in the salon, on an antique chaise longue, like a Victorian heroine from a third-rate novel. Above her as she woke were the faces of her mother and Zina. Zina's frowning concern brought back to Tala's mind all that had overwhelmed her in the bedroom, and she shut her eyes again, only to find her mother's pointed, burgundy-painted fingernail applied to her stomach.

'Stay awake, mama,' she exhorted. 'It's better for you.'

Tala doubted this to be true. On the contrary, the slip back into giddy blackness was more than appealing – it was seductive. It would be such sensual pleasure to glide away from Reema's poking finger, from Zina's intent perception, and to simply drift into the soothing darkness of sleep, where she would not have to think about what to tell Hani, how to tell him. She opened her eyes again and sat up, which was not easy against the assorted, solicitous hands that encouraged her back onto the sofa. She could now hear her father in the background, ordering mint tea, and she was grateful, for it struck her fractious mind as a good idea. Perhaps the scalding, soothing, sugary liquid could give her the sustenance she so desperately craved. Her mother got up, assuring her that she had just the thing to cure this kind of fainting spell upstairs in her bathroom. This left her with Zina, who held her hand tightly, while her father paced in the background.

'What is it, Tala?' Zina whispered. 'What happened?'

Tala swallowed. 'I'm not sure,' she lied. Her eyes went to her father, who cast glances of concern towards her. 'Zina, I need to talk to Baba. Alone.'

Zina nodded, and damped down her own curiosity, her own wish that Tala would confide in her, and left the room, closing the heavy door with a discreet click behind her.

Tala swung her legs off the sofa and tried to stand up, but Omar was next to her in a moment, guiding her down.

'Just sit a while. You've had a shock.'

Tentatively, he sat down opposite her and played with his watch strap while he waited for her to speak, but the silent moments dripped by, sitting heavily on him, and once he had checked every metal link of the watch and found each one satisfactory, he realized that he might have to open the conversation himself.

'I have a strange sense of déjà vu,' he offered. 'I feel we have been here before.'

Guiltily, Tala looked away. 'I'm sorry, Baba.'

Omar nodded, and stood up again to continue pacing.

'Tala, everyone gets nervous,' he said. 'It's normal. But sometimes you have to ignore it, keep moving till you get past it. If you are in love it will be okay.'

Tala stared at the floor. The polished wood, the edges of the Persian carpet that lay within her line of vision. She traced the patterns of the grain, the rich threads of the carpet with her eyes. Her lips parted, wanting to say something, to admit something, that she knew what it was to be in love, but that she wasn't in love with Hani.

'It's not nerves,' she said. 'You see, Baba, I don't love him. Not like I should. It's not that I'm not sure,' she continued, the words rushing out now. 'I wake up every morning suffocated by the idea of living here in Amman, of living with him, I realize now that I have been dreading my wedding day, every day. Dreading it.'

She had certainly spoken longer paragraphs to her father over the course of the years, but never one that held such frank emotion, and for a moment Tala blushed at what he must think of her. For she could not quite bring herself to look up and see for herself. Her eyes remained fixed on the floor, while she listened to the measured tread of his shoes, and saw the tops of them come into her eyeline, felt him standing over her. In the background, somewhere in a hallway, she could hear her mother's voice approaching.

'Go and tell Hani,' Omar said. 'Go before your mother comes. It will be okay.'

'I was hoping you'd surprise me,' Hani said. Taking her hand, he pulled her into his own office, away from the small reception area.

The building was large, recently renovated, but his small personal space comprised only a battered desk set amid peeling walls.

'They're painting it next week,' he said, following the flicker of her gaze. 'They should get your mother to interior design the whole place.'

He was smiling, and there was room for her to smile too, to add a laughing comment about how Reema would have him sit on a gilded chair at a cut glass table, but she could not lay out such banal banter now, when she was preparing to crush his expectations. Expectations that she had given him.

'What's wrong?' he asked as she sat down. He remained standing before her, leaning against his desk, his hand reaching out to touch her hair, to stroke it gently back from her forehead. 'Is it all getting too much?'

'Yes.' She was hanging inside a vacuum, the inside of an empty, comforting shell, facing an inexorable, relentless pull from the small window of opportunity she now saw before her. She wanted to turn and leave, but the inevitability of what was to come held her, and the pull of the rushing air from that window was sucking her towards what she had to say. She felt herself approach the sentence, felt her inner organs being dragged out of her as she put aside thought and just spoke.

'I'm not going to marry you,' she said. She stared at him, to see if he had heard. He had. His hand was removed from her head, and was held awkwardly against his stomach, as though shielding a gunshot wound. There was no room for maneouver amongst her words, no chink of daylight in the dark shutters she had just closed across his heart. The sentence was not ambivalent, the tone was not confused. She had decided, and it was already done.

'Why?' he asked, his voice hoarse.

'It doesn't feel right.'

He considered. 'Do you need more time? I don't even care about marriage,' he continued. 'We can leave this place and just live together, wherever you want.'

He was crying, he realised, and he blinked back the drops that were gathering thickly in his eyes.

'I don't want a wedding,' he said. 'I just want you.'

In these excruciating, elongated moments she found that she hated herself with a depth of feeling she had rarely experienced before. That her own self-deception and self-absorption, her own slavery to the society and family in which she had been brought up, had reduced this blameless man to a weeping wreck struck her as horrific. She saw more clearly than she had ever seen before that she must change, or keep hurting the people who truly loved her. Like Hani.

'Is there anything I can do to salvage this?' he asked, the rationality of his question lost under the desperate cracking of his voice.

'No. You haven't done anything to ruin it. I have. It's all my fault, and I am so sorry, Hani, so sorry that I couldn't be honest with you – and myself – sooner.'

'What is it? Have I done something?'

Tala looked at him. It would surely comfort him to know the true reason, to know that no matter what he did, he could never compete with the person she really wanted. But she could not bring herself to say it out loud, to admit it to anyone. There was still a sense of shame about the idea that clung to her like an old cobweb.

'I love you, Tala.'

'I love you too.'

'But not enough to marry me?' he asked angrily.

'Not in the right way,' she whispered.

She got up to hold him, and he submitted, but his grasp was hot and tense, until she pulled his head down to her neck, and he let out a ragged breath and stood there without moving for many minutes.

Reema was incandescent with a rage that, over the course of two hours, sublimated into hysterical grief at the demise of her own hopes. The air in the house now held the grey pallor of mourning. The sun still rammed with brilliant solidity against the glass; the crammed plant-life of the garden still let out the dense, vegetal smell of profuse growth. But within the rising walls of the home, all was death. The tight, angry shuffle that Reema used to ascend the staircase to her own room, the pursed, thin set of her lips, were the bitter signs of a woman forced to prepare for a funeral in the midst of a wedding.

Tersely, she ordered Rani to begin packing her daughter's bags, and plenty of them, for she intended to take Tala with her to London the next day for a good, long spell. She could not allow her to remain here to embarrass them even more, and the idea of sitting through visits from pitying, prying, probing friends was too much for Reema to bear.

The other three engagements were bad enough, but this. To break it off, to embarrass them all, to ruin everything the day before was unacceptable, and she would not accept it. She had to allow it – that much she was forced to admit – for, as usual, Omar was the weak link, had always been gentle at the times when the full force of his male strength and power was needed. Omar always sided with Tala when a crisis came to its apex – he would never force her to go through with an actual marriage; if he had, Tala would have discovered that marrying someone was no worse or better than a hundred other things she could decide to do with her day. But it was over; the union between Tala and Hani – handsome, good, perfect Hani – had been severed. She would never forgive it. Today was the day of her daughter's death, Reema decided, at least for the foreseeable future.

The yelling hawkers and tradesmen of downtown Amman provided a constant, staccato backdrop of screams for Hani's ears. He stood very still, with the sun casting its heavy heat onto the crown of his

head, and listened as they shouted the names and remarkable quali-
ties of the tired merchandise they tried to sell. He liked the souk, he
liked this area of the city. He would not live here unless he had to
– it was noisy, dirty and overcrowded – but he did not have the an-
tipathy towards it that many of his peers had. West Amman, where
he now lived, was a separate enclave, a faux town within the real
city. It had beautiful homes built on its cresting hills, and appealing
restaurants along its wider streets, but it lacked the life and heart of
downtown. The raw, urgent bawl of everyday life. He had grown
up near here before his father had made his fortune; his family not
poor enough to be stuck in the rotting centre of the souk, but not
yet rich enough to be very far removed from the competing wails of
the mosques and the roaring races of the delivery trucks along the
narrow roads where enough of the desert encroached to coat everything in fine dust. He loved this city, and she did not. He loved her
and she did not love him, not enough to pledge herself to him for a
lifetime. The world appeared simple for the traders out there; it was
a matter of survival or demise, selling enough to buy food and old
clothes, or starving. And it was now simple for him, who had no
such immediate concerns of hunger or want. There was light and
there was darkness, and where once, so recently, he had sat at his
desk bathed in that light, now he was clothed in the black cover of
heartbreak. He felt a pull at his sleeve. A young boy, thin and dirty,
grinned and offered up a bag of figs for sale.

'Fifty fils,' the boy said. Hani's eyes went to the fruit. Squashed
against the clear plastic of the bag, the figs were already blackened,
with soft patches where the skin had collapsed in against the dark
crimson of the flesh. He could smell the rotting odour of them from
where he stood.

'Okay, okay, thirty fils,' the boy compromised. He held up the
bag again, bringing the corrupted fruit closer to Hani's gaze. Hani
reached for the bag and cradled it in his hands. The squelching, bad
figs felt right in his hands. This was what he wanted to hold now

that she had slipped through his fingers. This was all that was left to him, and he could not yet begin to imagine how to rescue the rest of his life from the festering ruins of the fruit. The boy held out a demanding hand. Hani dipped into his pocket, pulled out two dinars and placed them in the outstretched palm.

'*Shukhran, Ammo,*' the delighted boy said. 'May Allah make you happy and give you all your dreams...'

Hani waved the child off, and the boy turned away, grinning. He watched as the thrilled child ran off towards his home, shouting and punching the air with delight.

Chapter 13

YASMIN ARRIVED BACK from her work trip a little after dinner time, but even at this hour, in a house not known for its late night bonhomie, she would have expected a few more lights on, and the low hum of the television. She walked in tentatively, half-expecting Maya to come at her with a rolling pin (that had happened once before, when she had tried to creep in at three in the morning), but there was nothing, no sign of life at all.

'I'm home!' she called out. But her voice echoed dully in the hall. Heading up the stairs, she passed by her parents' room, which was doused in complete darkness already, and stopped outside Leyla's, where a line of lamp light eased out from under the door.

'Hey!' said Yasmin, knocking gently. She waited a moment then opened the door and walked in. Leyla was sitting, immobile, at her desk, correcting something with a pencil. She glanced up only briefly, Yasmin noted, as she stalked about the room and then threw herself on the bed.

'What's happening in this house? I've seen mortuaries with more life.'

Leyla looked away from her work and out of the window. A man in a suit was getting into a car across the street; a cat jumped down into their front garden and padded softly over the grass. The gentle, suburban peace of the street felt calming and soothing. A street where no-one was gay. Or at least, no-one said anything about it.

'What is it?' Yasmin asked.

Leyla swung around in her desk chair to face her sister.

'Last night, I told Mum I'm gay and she threw a fit.'

Yasmin sat up on the bed. 'You're gay?'

'You knew,' Leyla replied.

Yasmin ran a hand over her eyes and supposed that to be true. But hearing it confirmed, from Leyla herself, still held some shock value. She tried to put that aside though, for there was evidently a parental wrong to be put right.

'Dad?' she asked.

'Dad walked in halfway through. He was sweet.'

Yasmin let out a low chuckle as she envisioned the scene.

'It's not funny,' Leyla said. 'Mum's acting like I stabbed her.'

'And you did,' Yasmin confirmed. 'You stuck a knife in her balloon. She had you down for a wedding next year...'

'Who with?'

'Who cares?' Yasmin shrugged. 'Can you marry Tala? Maybe that'll keep her happy.'

Leyla turned away, surprised by her sister's perception but also by hearing that name spoken aloud. She studied the pens and paper that were scattered over her desk.

'Tala has nothing to do with this. Anyway,' she added brightly. 'Someone else asked me out.'

'A girl?' gasped Yasmin.

'Yes, a girl,' said Leyla irritably.

Yasmin lay back on the bed to absorb this. 'I'm really happy for you Leyla. Seriously. I'm proud of you.'

Leyla swallowed, trying to push down the tears that edged up to her eyes. She was grateful for her sister, she realized, and relieved to have grasped the chance for honesty with her parents. Overwhelmed with a sentimental feeling of affection for Yasmin, she got up to go and hug her, but was halted mid-motion by a throaty laugh that emanated from the bed.

'What is it?'

Yasmin's shoulders shook as she tried to speak. 'All my life, as I snuck around with boyfriends, broke curfews, left home, took all that heat, I wondered. Will Leyla EVER do anything to piss off our parents?'

She reached up to wipe away tears as she rolled over, laughing so hard that for the first time in two days, Leyla smiled.

Tala's guilt over her treatment of Hani was tempered by an uncontrollable sense of release, of relief at having escaped, but as pleasurable as that was, she found herself feeling only more guilty for experiencing it. She had kept herself very busy during these first days back in London, had pushed herself back into her work, in order to lessen the time she had to feel anything at all. But when she walked across the park to meet Ali for a drink before a business dinner, she felt a light veil of shame wrap itself about her, even before they had greeted each other. Watching his lanky frame quicken its step towards her, watching his slow, spreading smile, it occurred to her for the first time that she had betrayed not just Hani but Ali too, ruthlessly. Those long, languid days of insanity that had occurred with Leyla had happened without Tala stopping to consider that she was attracted to – that she had slept with – Ali's girlfriend.

'Hey!' He greeted her with a customary hug, and then stopped to look at her intently. 'How are you? This must have been a tough few days for you.'

Tala swallowed and tried to smile.

'I'm fine. It's Hani I feel bad for.' She looked up at Ali, her eyes filled with dismay and pity, pity for him, that he must have misread, for he quickly put an arm around her shoulders and squeezed them reassuringly. They started walking. Their footfalls on the quiet path echoed into the clear night.

'You know you did the right thing, Tala. If he wasn't the one,' Ali said.

'I should have told him sooner,' she replied, and her voice was harsh, rough with anger at herself and with Ali for being so understanding when he should hate her. She looked up and noted a few stars glimmering gently. It was a rare sight in this city, so often pressed beneath a layer of cloud, and she stopped and looked up for a long moment, gathering herself. She took a breath, turned to him and smiled.

'What about you? How are you?'

'I'm fine.' he told her. 'Young, free and single!' He laughed.

'Single?' Tala hesitated. 'You're not seeing Leyla?' The taste of her name on Tala's tongue was soft and delicate, a fragile utterance that she did not want to give up to the cool night air.

'She dumped me.' Ali took in the shock on Tala's face and shrugged. 'I know, hard to believe,' he deadpanned, 'but at least it wasn't my fault. She told me she's gay.'

Tala stared at him, then looked away, remembering to close her mouth, which she realized was open in slack surprise. Ali nodded, sympathetic to his friend's reaction.

'I know. I was shocked too. Apparently, she even told her parents.'

'You're kidding,' Tala whispered.

'No. There's not many people in our community willing to do that. Got to admire her guts.' He gave a half-laugh, and when Tala looked at him, his eyes seemed wistful. 'She's always had a fierce streak. I liked that about her.'

He glanced at Tala for understanding, and she nodded slightly, an affirmation that he was right to feel the loss of Leyla. With a sigh, he started walking again, holding out a hand for Tala and she clasped it firmly, squeezing into her touch all the solace and all the silent apology that she could.

Tala walked quietly into her parents' living room when she returned, where only the otherworldly luminosity of the screen flickered in the darkened room, but the sound of her steps was enough to rouse Reema, whose coiffed head bobbed into view above the top of her favourite armchair, followed immediately by the yellow gasp of the lighter flame.

'Mama, you're late tonight,' Reema commented. Her voice was thick with sleep, Tala noted, as she walked in and stood before her mother's chair. Sure enough, Reema's heavy-lidded eyes peered at the television screen, their confusion betraying that she had lost the plot of the action some time ago.

'It was a business dinner. They liked my plans and the products. And I saw Ali.' Tala said, but her mother did not appear to be listening.

'This guy was in prison five minutes ago,' Reema complained, examining the television with dissatisfaction. 'Now he's out. They don't write proper stories these days,' she said. 'Stories about love. Who wants prison and shooting all the time?'

'Why don't you go to bed, mama?' Tala suggested. 'You look tired.'

Reema heard this last comment without a problem, for it touched on one of the subjects on which she was most sensitive – her appearance. 'Of course I'm tired. I'm worried all the time. You'd be tired, if you had my concerns.'

Reema regarded her daughter with rheumy, smoke-darkened eyes. Tala smiled briefly, then turned away. It was too late, too dark, too depressing to sit here and talk to her mother with only the neon flicker of the television lighting their awkward faces.

'I'm going to bed, I'm shattered,' Tala said, yawning slightly to lend credence to her statement. But Reema was already re-absorbed in the movie, and Tala was at liberty to make her escape to her own room, which she did swiftly and with as little noise as possible.

Once there, she shut the door, turned on lamps and opened the drawers of the plain, antique writing bureau that stood in the corner. The bureau was adorned with monogrammed stationary, heavy and rich to the touch, a fountain pen that her parents had given her one Christmas and a solid silver seal with her initials etched upon it, which had been a present from Lamia. She rarely used any of these items, except as decorative touches in an otherwise cleanly furnished room. The exposed wood, white paint and clean granite of her bedroom upstairs was very unlike the ornate, gilded melange of furnishings and decoration that encrusted her parents' world beneath.

She searched two drawers of the bureau without success, and was coming to terms with the fact that she really must have discarded Leyla's stories – for after her sudden departure and in the maelstrom of her own guilt over Hani, Tala had decided she must throw them out – when she found them folded and pushed into one corner of the bottom drawer, like shameful reminders of her past uncontrolled feelings. Methodically, Tala took them out, flattening the magazines on the top of the desk. Just reading the name printed beneath the titles caused a prickle of sensation, of elation, on her skin, that she wished she could stop, or could control, for she did not know if what lay behind it was something real, or a mere desperate imagining that had transformed a short, intense encounter into a meaningful relationship. It hardly mattered, because these stories were all that belonged to her, here and now, for she had walked away from the chance to be with the person behind them, and did not know if she would ever be forgiven.

Tala left the stories on the bed, and showered and changed, deliberately delaying the pleasure of reading them. Outside the soft pallor and quiet atmosphere of her bedroom, the life of the city continued unabated. There were police sirens and motorbikes, and Arabic music that issued from a car in the street far below. A rough accent broke the night air down there too, cursing drunkenly at a driver, and a couple passed by quickly, talking excitedly. Tala closed the window, sealing off the intensity of these sounds, and got into her bed. Its clean, ironed sheets felt coolly pleasurable to her warm skin and she lay there gratefully for a moment before reaching for the crumpled stack of paper.

Quickly, she read through them, hardly daring to hope that the stories would affect her as they originally had, but they did, perhaps even more so, for now Tala felt the prickle of tears in her eyes as she reached their sorrowful endings. Instinctively, she reached for the phone, and for Leyla's number, studiously ignored for too long in her address book. But it was almost midnight, and she had, after all, some sense of propriety. She would wait until morning, she decided, but then she would definitely call.

In a direct assault on her mother's funereal demeanour and the continued silence from her room, Yasmin descended the stairs early the next morning, before anyone was up and went straight to the kitchen radio which she switched on loudly enough to send a shiver through the china cups that Maya hung along the counter wall but never used. As she had hoped, her activity enticed her sister downstairs. Leyla came into the kitchen gingerly, checking for signs of their mother. Once she had ascertained that the coast was clear, she sniffed.

'What's that?'

'Real coffee,' said Yasmin, dancing around the kitchen to the music. 'I thought it was time we broke the tyranny of weak tea.'

Leyla smiled, and helped her sister bring cereals and cups to the table. Under the thrilling thump of the bass drums from the radio, only Yasmin heard the shrill ring of the phone, which she answered before holding out the handset to her sister.

'Who is it?' Leyla asked frowning.

'Tala,' mouthed Yasmin with a twinkle in her eye.

'I don't want to talk to her,' Leyla said, without thinking.

Yasmin turned around and made a few lascivious dance moves, before dropping to her knees and beating her chest while clutching her hair, a plea on Tala's behalf that left her sister unmoved. Leyla shook her head and turned away, sitting down at the table, back straight and unmoving, her hands rested flat against the wood as if touching it for support. Yasmin noted all of this, noted how her sister was straining to appear unconcerned about Tala. She frowned and put the phone back to her ear.

'Sorry, she can't come to the phone right now,' she said. With a sigh, she switched off the handset and turned the music back up.

Up in her room, Maya shifted uneasily. The thud of the music pumped up through her floorboards and was barely muffled by the heavy carpet. She had enjoyed her few days of self-pity sealed mainly in her room, as long as everyone else was sealed in theirs, but now the house, the kitchen was being taken over, and God knows what odd concoctions Yasmin would be trying to cook up in there. And, truth be told, she was getting weary of imagining the wedding she would never now attend. She got up from the bed, quickly put on a shirt and slacks and stomped downstairs where she found that everything was worse than she had imagined. There was music pounding away, if you could call that racket music, and the horrible stench of coffee everywhere. Maya reached to turn off the radio, with a disapproving flick of the wrist.

'How can you think straight with all that noise?' she demanded.

'Apparently, Leyla can't think straight at all,' Yasmin snorted.

Maya glared at her daughter. She didn't quite understand what she had just said, but she could sense it had something to do with Leyla and her affliction. Lips pursed, Maya made her way to the kettle which was cold, she noted, casting her gaze at the strange metal coffee pot that stood bubbling on the stove.

Leyla gave her sister a sign to ease off. She wanted to handle this more persuasively; she would rather spend repetitive and achingly slow hours attempting to change Maya's perception, than charge in to war and face months of tiny battles, which would play themselves out on the most remote fields of engagement, such as how she did her laundry, whether she ate at home often enough, or used the telephone too much. But Yasmin seemed in no mood to heed anybody's wishes.

'You know, Mum, this is not Leyla's fault. She hasn't done anything wrong. And yet you're treating her like a leper.'

'Oh! So I am to blame,' Maya said. 'Of course I am. I am good for nothing in this house but to be a scapegoat.'

Yasmin sighed and sat down at the table, sorrowfully realizing that the anticipated moment of bliss with her coffee and croissant was all but over. Maya left the kettle boiling and reached for the remote control, carefully aimed the end of it directly at the tiny red spot at the base of the small television that she kept on the counter, then spent a good twenty seconds locating the correct button before pressing it. The exaggerated attention to this simple act, this elevating of a mundane movement into a technological event irritated Yasmin further, but she resisted putting out her hand for the remote control. In her current mood, her mother would not give it up easily.

'Mum, can we just discuss this?' Leyla began, but Maya's eyes were fixed doggedly on the screen which displayed a talk show panel made up of the wives of cross-dressing husbands. Yasmin cast a glance at the television and snorted again, struggling to contain a mouthful of coffee through her mirth, while Maya felt the pinpricks of tears in her eyes, a manifestation of her sorrow that nowhere in this world was she safe from the tentacles of depravity. Maya repeated the achingly slow process with the remote control in reverse, and in the profound quiet that ensued, looked at Leyla.

'Why are you doing this to me?'

Yasmin turned on her mother. 'She's not doing anything, she *is* gay. It's not a choice. So I think, actually, that you should be telling us why you have such a problem with it.'

Leyla knew that her chance of avoiding the stress of hand to hand combat with her mother had evaporated with this last speech, but she applauded it inwardly all the same. She looked at her sister, lanky, beautiful, her eyebrows drawn in with concern and anger, her arms folded loosely in an attitude of complete self-assurance.

Maya needed time to think. On the one hand she could indulge her instinctive response, which was to bemoan the fact that after all her years of nurturing and care, this was the way her daughters chose to speak to her. No respect, no decency, nothing. She went through the speech in her head, and derived from it the sweet sap of instant satisfaction, which was made all the more delicious by the fact that her ungrateful daughters could not answer back. Having accomplished that immediate gratification, she turned her attention to Yasmin, and found that she had nothing to say. All she could feel was fear, sitting in her chest like a ball of steel. She was fifty-two years old, and had done nothing except raise these children and support her husband. That was work enough – she had certainly complained about it almost daily for the past quarter of a century, and now, her one reward, the prize she had anticipated with such relish for so long, the wedding, would no longer be taking place. Without it, without the preparations and shopping and congratulations and general elevation of status amongst her peers at the mosque, she could not imagine what else would be left for her when Leyla was in lesbian bars picking up girls, and Yasmin was, God forbid, backpacking somewhere on the subcontinent. Sam was more and more immersed in his work, it never ended, and only seemed to get worse even as she nagged him to slow down and spend more time with her. And she would not know what her daughters were doing, nor whom they were doing it with. They would be away, alone, learning things she had never considered from books she had never heard of. They would be completely out of her sphere of influence. She shut her eyes briefly and considered how best to encapsulate all that she felt into one, comprehensible sentence.

'What do two women do together?' she said. And at once, the dropping of her shoulders, the lowering of her own, confused, angry eyes, held the ache of failure – that she could never truly say what she meant. Yasmin shook her head and sighed while Leyla touched her mother's shoulder with a gentleness that Yasmin felt was overly kind and not in the least warranted.

'Knit?' offered Yasmin. 'Make jam?'

'It's not natural,' Maya offered.

'Jam-making? I agree. Not when you can buy a decent jar for a couple of quid. All that peeling and boiling. And what is pectin anyway?' Yasmin looked to her mother and sister for confirmation and found them both trying not to smile. She pushed a coffee cup in front of Maya.

'Here, try this,' she said. 'It's time to broaden your horizons, Mum.'

Maya sighed with annoyance, and sniffed at the cup as if it might be arsenic, but after a short moment, conscious of her daughters' eyes upon her, she picked it up and sipped at it, if only so she could have the satisfaction of telling them how bad it tasted.

Chapter 14

Tala kept the phone pressed to her ear, and listened once again to the room tone of Leyla's house, as though it might hold a clue to the future. Twice in the past few days she had spoken to a polite voice on the other end (once her sister, once her father) and each time they had confirmed that Leyla was there, before coming back on the line to say that she was busy.

'Hello?' The father's voice was back, not a good sign. 'She's tied up with something right now,' he said.

'Thank you. I'll call again,' said Tala. She waited for the final click of the receiver to cut the line at the other end, waited for the ugly, cold blare of the dial tone. She should have asked for their address, she realized, because she was now faintly aware that she could not call again, not after such emphatic and obvious rejection three times, not without veering into the domain of stalkers.

Quickly, summoning all her reserves of energy, she walked past her bed, which looked so inviting. It would take only a second to drop down onto it, to curl up between the duvet and the pillows and close her eyes and think about Leyla, or better yet, fall asleep and forget about her. She moved on, into the bathroom, and stripped off her clothes, turning on the shower, waiting for the heated water to flow through. She watched herself in the mirror for a moment as she recalled Oxford, recalled their night together, that night of insanity and reality. She shook herself, tied back her hair and stepped under the soothing rivulets of water. She was due across London in two hours to attend a lecture, and still had work to do in the meantime.

'Perhaps one of the most stunning archeological finds of that century, indeed, any century, was that of the lost city of Petra. Carved out of rose-coloured stone by the Nabateans, the city has become a symbol of Jordan's history and its beauty…'

Tala opened her eyes and tried to focus on the lecturer. A few moments of closing her eyes could be interpreted as concentration or deep thought, but allowing the warm darkness to lull her to sleep could only be interpreted as rudeness, particularly when she was representing her family. The lecture series had been such a success in Oxford over the summer that it was being repeated in London. The speaker was warm and funny and had evidently captivated everyone else in the audience, but it was the fourth time Tala had heard about the wonders of Jordan, and she amused herself by taking in the intricate, wood-panelled carving of the grand hall in which she sat, in the midst of about twenty rows of people. She watched some of them, the ones she could take in by shifting her glance sideways without turning her head. They seemed interested, polite. There were many older people and more men than women, and there, about five rows in front of her, a girl who looked exactly like Leyla… Tala's heart jumped and she stopped and looked down to compose herself. It was not the first time she had thought she had seen Leyla in an odd place. Once she had caught a glimpse of silken dark hair and skin and had actually run down a busy street towards it, certain that it was Leyla at the other end, getting into a cab, only to find as she bore down on the taxi, that the girl in question – a stranger to her – had turned in fear of being mugged by a sprinting, curly-haired maniac.

She looked up now, and shifted a little in her seat, to get a better line of vision. She peered hard at the back of the head, at the set of the shoulders, both of which seemed so much like her that it caused Tala's breathing to quicken. And then, the girl turned, she turned to the woman sitting beside her and whispered something in her ear, and they both smiled, and it was Leyla. Tala craned her neck to see something of the girl Leyla was with, but at that moment, the lecture ended and amid the applause, people began to stand up. Swiftly, Tala vacated her seat and made for the door. What she would do, she didn't know, but something about the intimacy of that glance between Leyla and her friend had set her teeth on edge, and she could not stay around to see more of it.

'Apparently you can only get into Petra on a horse. Or a camel,' Leyla said as she descended the sweeping marble steps outside the lecture hall.

'I'd like to see you on a camel,' returned Jennifer. 'Maybe we should go.' Leyla smiled back at the sparkling blue eyes and considered how it might be to take a trip away with her new girlfriend.

'Maybe we should.' It was a step forward for her, and she saw the pleasure in Jennifer's smile, and was wondering if she could kiss her right here, as they turned the corner of the staircase, when she felt the grasp of a hand on her arm. Leyla paused, looking up in surprise and found Tala standing there. She realized at once that she had already begun to forget the exact planes of her face and her features. That Tala looked more beautiful than she had remembered, but also different, less like the idealized image that Leyla had nurtured in her mind and more like a real person. She looked away from the hazel eyes that watched her and found her gaze on the soft hollow of Tala's throat, where she had rested her lips once. Leyla tried to breathe more deeply, for she could feel her heart hammering in her chest, was worried that everyone could hear it as the echoing clatter of the footsteps around her, all the talk, all the chatter faded away. She remained painfully conscious of Jennifer, standing behind her.

'What are you doing here?' Leyla asked, moving her arm away from Tala's grip.

'My family sponsored the lecture,' Tala replied. 'What are you doing here?'

Leyla cleared her throat, which was unaccountably hoarse.

'I'm interested in Jordan.'

'It has a population of five million and no natural resources to speak of. Petra's lovely, but there really isn't much to say about Jordan,' Tala stated before hesitating perceptibly. Her voice dropped. 'It's me you're interested in.'

Leyla felt the sting of embarrassment touch her cheeks, embarrassment that Jennifer had heard this, and embarrassment at Tala's intuition. Certainly, there were one hundred other things she could have chosen to do on this Saturday afternoon in this city than attend a lecture about this particular country. Her eyes flickered away, to the marble floor beneath her feet, where they lingered to gather strength before coming up to meet Tala's gaze again, pointedly.

'How was your wedding?' she asked, trying to mask an undertone of bitterness.

The relief that coursed through Tala at being asked this question, the question which she had longed to be asked by Leyla, made her almost light-headed. She tried to stop a smile coming to her lips as she opened her mouth to reply.

'I...'

'Leyla, let's go,' Jennifer interrupted.

Tala dragged her eyes away from Leyla to cast a savage gaze at the girl behind her. She was pretty, Tala noted, but seemed to have an attitude. Leyla followed the look.

'This is my friend, Jennifer,' she said politely. Tala noted that the 'friend' was holding out a hand, and she felt her stomach turn as she watched Leyla's hand reach back, slowly, and take it. Tala stared at the hands, together, joined, entangled. Leyla's slim fingers that she had once held in her own, that she had kissed, and felt caress her face, her back, her thighs, her breasts.

'Your friend?' demanded Tala, in a tone that she was dimly aware was inappropriate, but which she could no longer control.

'Her girlfriend,' Jennifer clarified helpfully, and she tugged at Leyla, and Leyla turned and began to walk down the stairs with her, leaving Tala behind, leaving her standing there. She waited, without moving, until the echo of their steps had disappeared completely, until the low undertones of their discussion ('Who was that?' 'Oh just someone I used to know') had receded into the background hum of the traffic outside.

There was half an hour to spare before she had to meet Ali, so she ignored the cabs that drove past her, a couple of them slowing down, expecting to pick up a fare from the well-dressed girl walking along the street, for it was raining hard. The droplets felt jagged on her head as she walked, and began to seep into even the resistant cloth of her jacket, but she continued on, head down against the wind-driven angle of the rain, so that she could see nothing of the majestic brick edifices around her, could not even take comfort from the low sodium light of the newly lit street lamps. What she wanted now was the heavy weight of the cold water soaking her clothes, the metallic smell of the city rain lying sodden in her hair.

She did not feel like seeing Ali, she felt like being alone, but she walked on, without haste, to their rendezvous, for this was also what she wanted now. It was right to have to sit there and remember how she had betrayed him, even while he was kind enough to try to make her laugh or smile, anything to pull her out of the sorrow that he would sense in her. She reached the restaurant a few minutes early, but he was already there waiting. Hastily, aware now that she was dripping on things, she took off her coat.

'You know they have these amazing inventions called cars. And buses. And taxis,' Ali told her.

'I felt like the walk.'

She stood there, feeling the water from her hair drip onto her nose and down to her chin. She shook it away, embarrassed suddenly, under his practical gaze, unable to explain why she was behaving so strangely.

Ali shook his head and smiled, and she noticed that they were sitting alone at a table for eight. He followed her eyes.

'I have a few friends joining us,' he explained

'Who?' she asked, trying to hide her annoyance.

'Jeff and a couple of others. Leyla said she'd come,' he added, persuasively. 'I haven't seen her in ages. We could all catch up.'

'You know, I'm really tired. I need an early night.' She couldn't look at him, so she looked at the waiter, and asked for her coat.

'What are you doing? Tala?'

She had no idea what to say, or how to explain her bizarre behaviour. She only knew that she could not, unless heavily sedated, and possibly not even then, sit at a dinner table with Leyla and her girlfriend and watch them touch each other, feed each other, look at each other.

'I'm sorry. I don't feel that great. I think I'm coming down with a cold,' she said, edging out of her seat.

'Because you just got soaked..have some tea or something, you'll feel better…'

But Tala was already kissing his cheek.

'I'm sorry, Ali,' she said, and she paused against him for a moment, and touched his cheek gently, where a slight evening stubble roughened her fingers. She pulled back to look in his eyes. 'I really am sorry.'

'Hey, it's only a dinner,' he smiled. But she was already gone.

Chapter 15

YASMIN WAS PERTURBED to find that the pasta dough she had been kneading for ten minutes resolutely refused to become smooth and elastic. She continued kneading with an unabated enthusiasm though, because it gave her something else to focus on, something other than the phone call she was now stuck in.

At the time, she had thought that calling Ali to discuss her plan would be fun. She liked him, he had a good sense of humour, and a part of her relished the shock value of what she wanted to tell him. But when she had heard his voice she had felt a rush of affection, mixed with just a little pity, and she had not wanted to just come out with it.

'What I'm trying to say,' she began again 'is that love is a strange thing. Sometimes it springs up where you least expect it. You can't control it. And I think you just have to act on it. Encourage it.'

There was a long pause at the other end, during which Yasmin cradled the phone on her shoulder and got on with her kneading.

'Are you in love with me?' Ali asked, and she could hear the smile on his face, but also the underlying confusion in his tone.

'Well, you are cute, but this is not about me,' Yasmin said dryly. 'I want to get Tala and Leyla together, and I need your help.'

'But why?'

'Why what?' she asked, trying to force a modicum of patience into her tone as she fed dough into the pasta machine.

'Why do you want to get them together? The other night I suggested it and Tala didn't seem interested at all... In fact, it feels like she wants to avoid Leyla for some reason. No idea why.'

Yasmin sighed. 'Listen, did you ever see the TV show, "The L Word"?'

'No, but did you ever consider not speaking in riddles?' Ali shot back.

Yasmin took a breath and let her next words tumble out in a mess. 'They're in love with each other.'

'Who?'

Yasmin rolled her eyes at her uncut ravioli. 'Leyla and Tala.'

She waited. Clearly, he had understood at last, because there was no further sound from Ali, only the background noise of his phone.

'Ali, I....'

'I'll call you later,' he interrupted quietly and hung up the phone.

When Leyla had turned and walked away from Tala that afternoon after the lecture, she had felt a momentary sense of relief that she had Jennifer's protective hand to hold onto, that she could show Tala how she had moved on with her life, that she had not let Tala's marriage affect her. There was a tinge of pride too, she had to admit, in demonstrating that she, at least, would remain honest about who she really was. But both pride and relief were subsumed all too quickly beneath a much heavier sense of loss and she had made an excuse about not feeling well in order to avoid going back to Jennifer's flat. She could not think of Jennifer now, and she did not want to encourage an intimacy that would allow her to close her eyes and imagine Tala while she was with someone else.

And so for the past three days she had stayed at home, except for her hours in the office, which were becoming fewer as she prepared for the upcoming publication of her book. The idea of the book thrilled her but she came to realize that the low hum of excitement that quivered constantly in her body was somehow more related to Tala, to having seen her and felt the touch of her hand on her arm, and having caught the scent of her that she had forgotten.

In her robe, Leyla walked into the kitchen, past Yasmin who was doing something odd to a bowl of prawns, and through to a small laundry room, where her mother was applying a hot iron to her father's shirt. The room was warm, with curls of steam that settled around the windows' edges, and a welcoming light that pushed away the creeping dusk outside.

Maya looked up and held out her hand for the black dress that Leyla held over her arm.

'I can do that for you.' she said. 'You haven't worn a dress in ages.'

'I'm going out.'

'Who with?' Maya asked automatically, and then instantly regretted asking. She had made a point of never asking such things since Leyla's unfortunate revelation, because if she didn't ask, she wouldn't have to find out things she'd rather not know. But here, lulled into drowsiness by the warmth and the slow, rhythmic shift of the iron, she had lowered her guard and forgotten. She dropped her eyes back to the fabric before her.

'Ali asked me to have dinner with him,' Leyla replied.

Maya looked up, alert. This was news.

'He's a lovely boy,' she began.

'Mum! He's a friend.'

Maya bit her tongue against articulating her belief that a good friendship was what real marriages were all based on anyway, and went back to making sure the dress was ironed perfectly. Perhaps if he actually saw her looking like a girl, Maya thought, Ali would sweep her off her feet and at the same time sweep away this whole sorry phase of Leyla's life. She handed Leyla the dress and she slipped it on, twirling around for approval. Maya smiled.

Yasmin appeared at the doorway, car keys dangling in her hand, and let out a low wolf whistle at her sister's appearance.

'You should wear that for Gay Pride,' she advised Leyla, mainly for their mother's benefit. 'They'd eat you alive.'

'She's having dinner with Ali,' snapped Maya.

'Oh, I'm so pleased,' grinned Yasmin. 'He's such a good boy…'

'Where are you going?' Maya demanded.

'I'm going out,' Yasmin replied helpfully.

Maya sniffed at the lack of detail, the lack of respect, then she switched off the iron and chased Yasmin and Leyla away from the door and followed them into the kitchen where a massive pot of water was boiling away, steaming up the whole room.

'I made you and Dad homemade pasta with shrimp for dinner,' Yasmin explained.

'If I want a sauna, I can join a health club,' Maya said disconsolately, and turned, ready to face Yasmin's inevitable retort, only to find her youngest child regarding her with new respect.

'That was quite funny, Mum.'

'Someone answer the door,' Maya instructed, for the bell had rung, but her daughters might have been deaf for all the interest they showed. Yasmin obeyed, returning with a large, long gift box which she handed to Leyla.

Leyla stood awkwardly by the stove in the soft folds of her black dress with her mother and sister watching and gingerly removed the lid to reveal an expansive, spreading bouquet of long-stemmed red roses. On top lay a fine envelope upon which her name was inscribed in a deep blue ink.

'Ali?' breathed Maya.

'Jennifer?' suggested Yasmin.

'Tala,' whispered Leyla.

They all looked at each other, embarrassed in their own way, then Maya turned to put on the kettle for her tea, Yasmin left to go out, and Leyla took her present upstairs.

In the sanctuary of her own room, Leyla switched on lamps and sat down to open the letter. A thin, crisp sheet of paper emerged, as translucent and delicate as a petal, but there was no letter, no introduction and no signature, only a poem:

Every night I empty my heart, but by morning it's full again.
Slow droplets of you seep in through the night's soft caress.
At dawn, I overflow with thoughts of us,
An aching pleasure that gives me no respite.
Love cannot be contained, the neat packaging of desire
Splits asunder, spilling crimson through my days.
Long, languishing days that are now bruised tender with yearning,
Spent searching for a fingerprint, a scent, a breath you left behind.

Leyla brushed away the tears that sat thickly on her lashes. She hated Tala for doing this to her – for she knew it was Tala who had sat down and chiseled out that poem, who had crafted it and polished it for her alone. But why? It was late, too late. Leyla folded the poem gently along the delicate creases of the paper and slipped it under her pillow. Then she looked at the flowers, boldly crimson and exquisitely tinged with pink around the edges, a symbol of perfect beauty and perfect love. On an impulse, she picked up the lid of the box and closed them over, ready to give away, for they represented a world that did not truly exist, and she did not want a reminder of it too near her.

'Reservation for Ali, seven thirty?'

Leyla gathered herself as the waiter consulted his book. The drive into London had given her time to recover a little, and she felt stronger now, a little self-conscious in the unaccustomed dress, but a little more confident also. She was glad she had worn it, for Ali had chosen an exceptional restaurant.

'The other party hasn't arrived yet, Madam. Can I offer you a drink at the bar, or shall I show you to the table?'

Leyla glanced over at the bar, all polished wood and clinking crystal glasses, but it was dominated by an odd-looking woman dressed in a wide-brimmed floppy hat that fell over the huge dark glasses shielding her face. Probably an actress, Leyla thought; there was definitely something familiar about her.

'The table, please,' she asked, and followed the waiter inside. The floppy hatted woman's head turned to watch her as she went.

Tala waited in agony and in vain for any sign that Leyla had received the poem, and then, half an hour before she had to leave, started to get dressed. She did not have a clear idea of why Ali had insisted on inviting her to dinner, but she understood vaguely that it must be something to do with her wild-eyed, rain-sodden appearance and sudden disappearance the other night. She had made an effort to dress up a little, partly because the place he had booked was a very good one, but mostly to reassure him that there was nothing wrong with her.

She was not surprised when the waiter advised her that her dinner partner was already waiting – he was habitually early and she appreciated that about him, that he would prefer to wait than keep anyone waiting. She glanced at the gracious, old bar as she walked past, and felt the eyes of a strange woman in big sunglasses (at night!) and a big hat follow her as she passed. Tala shook off the self-consciousness that this moment induced and followed the waiter to the table.

Leyla had chosen that moment to unravel a napkin, which seemed to have been folded by an origami master, and so failed to notice that the waiter was leading someone to her table until she looked up to find Tala standing before her. She blinked, surprised, and saw her own confusion mirrored on Tala's face.

'I guess we've been set up,' Tala offered, uncertainly.

'So it seems.'

The chair was being held for her, and in the pause that followed, and not without a feeling of presumption, Tala sat down.

'The gentlemen sends his regrets, ladies,' the waiter said, handing them menus. 'But he wishes you a pleasant evening at his invitation.'

Tala was very warm suddenly, her face felt flushed, and she reached for the bottle of water that stood in an ice bucket beside them. After she had taken a sip, she looked at Leyla.

'You look wonderful,' she said.

'So do you.'

'I know,' Tala replied, deadpan. And Leyla laughed. Taking a breath, Tala smiled and felt a small measure of relief.

Out in the bar, a pretty young woman in a big hat and sunglasses paid for her drink, made a mental note never to order a watermelon martini ever again, and left.

Leyla knew that there was no way she could make small talk for very long, but she surprised even herself when, during the very first short pause in their early conversation she asked Tala how her husband was.

'I don't have one,' was the reply.

Leyla tried to look surprised (this was not hard, as the news did take her aback) but she tried also to stifle her other natural response, which was to laugh and punch the air. With a quiet dignity, achieved in part by staring hard at the butter dish, she waited for Tala to explain.

'I called off the wedding. The day before the wedding,' Tala said.

Clearly that kind of dramatic gesture deserved some response.

'That must have been very hard,' suggested Leyla.

'It was the second-hardest thing I've ever had to do,' Tala said, her eyes fixed intently on Leyla's. Now Leyla blushed, for she could divine Tala's meaning, not that she intended to let it go unarticulated.

'What was the first?'

Tala looked away and smiled, then glanced back at Leyla.

'Leaving you to go back to Jordan.'

Leyla smiled. Picking up her glass, she took a sip of wine. The taste spread lightly over her tongue and made her light-headed at once. Except that it was her first drink, and the giddiness could not be so easily blamed upon that alone.

Giving the taxi driver a huge tip, the woman in the floppy hat made her way past a crowd of after-work drinkers standing on the street, and into a much louder bar where the thumping beats made her shimmy slightly across the room, stopping with an upbeat wiggle in front of Ali. He looked a little tired and somewhat tense, she noted, as if he had been waiting for some time. Swiftly, Yasmin removed her glasses and hat.

'Well, I'm glad to see you were discreet,' Ali noted.

Yasmin grinned and shook out her hair, which had been pinned beneath the hat, and watched as he poured her some wine.

'And? How'd it go?' he asked, impatiently.

'There eyes met,' Yasmin said, pausing for dramatic effect. 'A brief smile played across Tala's mouth. Unconsciously, Leyla licked her lips…It's all over.'

Ali winced and downed the remains of his drink. 'You know, I'm still getting used to the idea,' he told her.

'Would it help if I drew you a diagram?'

'Definitely not,' Ali replied quickly. 'But it might help – a bit – if you had dinner with me now.'

'Don't want to be alone to brood about Leyla?' she asked, trying to be understanding. For she liked him, he was funny and intelligent and kind. How many men would set their ex-girlfriend up with their best friend? He was looking at her now, thoughtfully, and it felt a little too long before he answered, but when he did, she felt that he really meant what he said.

'It's not that,' he said. 'I'd just like to have dinner with you. That's all. I know nothing about you except that you clearly love your sister a lot, and that you make a great Greek salad…'

Yasmin smiled.

'I can't believe your book is being published!' Tala said. 'I mean, of course I can believe it, it's just that..'

To stop herself tripping over her own tongue, Tala reached out for Leyla's hand and squeezed it. An expression of her pride, her excitement. And now that their hands were together, it felt too wonderful to break apart. Lightly, as nonchalantly as possible, Tala held onto the long fingers, but after a short moment, Leyla pulled gently away. Tala touched her hair, conscious of the rejection and changed the subject.

'How's your girlfriend?'

'Jennifer?'

Tala cleared her throat. 'Has there been more than one?'

'No,' Leyla smiled. 'She's fine. Thanks for asking.'

'Do you love her, Leyla?'

Tala saw Leyla sit back slightly, perhaps because she herself was leaning forward now, earnest, demanding, as if this girl owed her any explanations when she clearly did not.

'There are things I love about her.'

Now Tala sat back; the sting of being hit with her own words about Hani had struck her off-balance. Casually, she glanced at the tables next to them, followed the steps of a passing waiter, listened to the subdued, well-bred laughter from a table behind her.

'And is that good enough for you?' she asked softly. She held Leyla's eyes now, would not let them shift away or find time to close off. Leyla shook her head, mutely, and Tala saw that she was on the verge of tears. Gently, she reached out her hand to touch Leyla, her cheek, her arm, anything to reassure her, to comfort her, but something indefinable snapped in the girl opposite. She pulled back and Tala saw at once that there was a new determination in her clear, dark eyes.

'What is it?' Tala asked.

'Did you tell your parents why you broke off the wedding?'

Tala saw the hole looming and she danced around it. 'I told them it wouldn't be fair to Hani.'

'Did you tell them why?'

The insistence, the stubborn need to push at things she didn't understand needled Tala intensely. Irritated, she pushed away her plate.

'Look, Leyla, you don't understand. The Middle East is an unforgiving place. And my parents have a strong presence in that world, and it's a culture that doesn't change...'

'And as long as people don't dare to be truthful about who they are, it never will change.'

Tala leaned forward. 'Leyla, I love you. Why should that be anyone else's business? Even my family's?'

Leyla had a good answer for this too, but it was temporarily lost to her as she tried to recover from hearing Tala utter the three words that she now realized she had longed to hear for so long. She marveled at how these three, ancient, hackneyed and probably overused monosyllables, strung together by the right person at the right moment, could change her world. And yet, Tala did not feel able to explain that feeling, that love, to anyone else. It would remain hidden, illicit, unreal.

'I don't want to lie about who I'm with and why I'm with them,' Leyla said. 'I don't want you to be my lover at home and my 'friend' everywhere else. I can't live like that.'

She saw Tala look away, sliding out from under her gaze, wishing this conversation did not have to happen.

'You know, you once told me to be more at ease with myself,' Leyla said quietly. 'Now I'm telling you the same thing.'

Tala tried to think of a reply, something that would explain why she could not do what Leyla expected, something to make her understand that just being in love with each other and together would be enough, but she realized with disbelief that it was too late. Leyla was standing up, gathering her bag and her things, and she was leaving.

'Don't..' Tala whispered, and Leyla stopped next to her chair and pressed her lips against her hair in a kiss that felt urgent and final. Then she turned and walked out of the restaurant, leaving Tala floating in an acid state of shock and bitter regret.

Chapter 16

IT WAS STRANGE AND UNEXPECTED that by the time she got home that night, Tala found herself thinking much more about Hani than Leyla. She let herself into the house, which stood quiet and softly lit. Rani, the housekeeper, heard the click of the front door from the kitchen where she had just boiled the kettle. Recognising Tala's steps, she poured the steaming water into a spotlessly clean cup which held a bag of herbal tea, then padded out to meet her at the foot of the stairs.

'Hi, Rani. Where are my parents?'

'Went out for dinner, Miss. Here, this is for you.'

Tala took the cup gratefully. 'Camomile. Thank you.'

'You're welcome, Miss,' Rani said, kindly.

'Any calls for me?'

She hoped that perhaps Leyla would have telephoned, that she would have in fact found herself unable to live without Tala, even in the half hour that had elapsed since she had left the restaurant.

'Nothing, Miss.' Rani hesitated. 'I'm sorry.'

Tala shook off the sympathy with a quick smile, and trudged upstairs. There were times when she felt her mother's laconic housekeeper knew more than anyone else about everything that went on in the house.

Gently, Tala closed the door to her room, and sat on the edge of her bed, in the dark, and thought about the evening that had begun so well and with such promise. She tried to trace the weaving line of the conversation, to pinpoint what had broken the delicate thread of their flirtation and she came back once more to her own words: 'I told them it wouldn't be fair to Hani.'

It had seemed like the truth at the time, at the apex of the wedding crisis. It had contained the correct amount of self-blame, and even held the suggestion that splintering the engagement would be more beneficial to him than to her. But now it felt like only a glossy-surfaced excuse that did not touch the reasons beneath. Leyla's insistence had stirred up in Tala a new kind of guilt towards her ex-fiancé.

Resolutely, without switching on lights, she reached for the phone and tapped in the familiar number.

'Hello?'

'Hani? It's me. Is this a bad time?'

She meant the question in the most practical way. To ask if he was in the middle of a meal, or asleep. But the length of his silence reminded her that there could never be a good time for him to hear again the voice he had been in love with.

'No, it's fine,' Hani said at last. 'Is everything okay?'

'Yes.'

He waited for more, for the reason why she was calling, but only a soft silence hung between them, as fragile as a spider's web.

'Hani, I have to tell you something,' Tala began. She swallowed and held her hand to her forehead as she spoke, for her palm felt cool and calming on the hot skin. She could feel him waiting for her to speak, and she opened her mouth to try but she couldn't.

'Tala, you don't owe me anything,' he said, and his tone was not harsh, but was not kind either. There was a weariness to his voice that pierced her. She looked up to the windows, where thin slats of yellow light from the street poked in through the shutters and threw long slashes of brightness across the wooden floor.

'I never told you why I didn't marry you, Hani. Not exactly. And I'd like to.'

'Go ahead,' he replied and she closed her eyes against even the shards of light from outside. Perhaps if it was so dark that she could not even catch the shadow of herself, she would be able to say it.

'Hani, I've always been more attracted to women than men. Always. And so, even though I loved you, I wasn't in love with you, not the way I am with...' Tala cut herself off and took a breath. 'What I mean is, I realised I did feel that way about someone, and it was Leyla. But I was too scared to admit it to myself, never mind to anyone else.'

She knew he was listening because she could hear him breathing, could hear him clear his throat.

'Wow,' he said. Then, after a long pause and a cough, a touch of irony: 'So it really wasn't my fault?'

She laughed, a little, and the release of the breath brought up tears, and to her chagrin, she could not find a way to stop them this time, they pooled up without concern for propriety or form and she cried, as silently as she could, while Hani listened without speaking. When she had finished, and was fumbling in the dark for the tissues that were next to her bed, she tried to apologise but he interrupted.

'You should be proud of yourself, Tala,' he said. 'For admitting it eventually. Not many people do. Especially from our part of the world. And..I'm glad you told me. It helps. Really, it does.' The lightness that he tried for could not rise above the heaviness of his tone, but she was grateful for his kindness, so grateful for his friendship.

'Tala, you can count on me to be totally discreet about this. You know that, don't you? I won't tell a soul.'

She wiped her nose and smiled. 'Well, maybe not for a day or two. I need to talk to my parents first,' she said, and he laughed, a throaty, happy sound this time.

'Good for you. And good luck,' Hani said. 'Because trust me, *habibti*, you are going to need it.'

Tala walked into the dining room at ten the following morning to find her parents in an expansive mood after a good dinner the night before and an excellent end to the evening for Reema in the casino. They greeted her with enthusiasm and ushered her in to join them for breakfast – a platter of tropical fruits which Reema steered solicitously towards her daughter.

'Have some papaya, mama,' Reema advised as she lit up a cigarette. 'It's anti-cancer.'

Tala considered whether she should point out the obvious irony as she watched the recommended fruit suffer under the pall of Reema's exhaled smoke, but her mother pre-empted her.

'Don't complain,' she said. 'I need a cigarette to get my system going in the morning.'

'I wanted to talk to you both,' Tala said quickly, composing herself.

Reema inhaled deeply, narrowing her eyes to regard her daughter.

'Whatever you have to tell us can't be good, or you would be smiling.'

There would be no need for small talk, Tala realised. The gate had been opened to her, and she had only to march through it.

'It is good,' she started boldly, determined not only to unload the basic premise, but to actively present it in a way that might possibly influence their reaction. 'I'm in love with a wonderful person.'

Omar frowned, while Reema bit on her cigarette holder. She prided herself that she always looked on the bright side of life, that she could find hope even where there seemed only to be despair – it was how she had gotten through life with two such disappointing children as Tala and Zina. But she knew in her heart that this opening was not good.

For some years now, Reema had vaguely sensed something about her eldest daughter, something that had made her regret her intractable insistence that her daughter attend a girls-only boarding school. Something horrible, something obscene, something disgusting. It was a mere suggestion, a possibility, a hunch, a sour taste on the back of her tongue, never something that she would spit up for everyone to see. Instead, Reema's strategy had been to keep swallowing it back down to the pit of her stomach whenever it appeared or, as in the recent case in Oxford with that girl Leyla, to arrange things so that a gentle pressure kept her daughter on the correct path.

'I'm gay,' Tala said, and she closed her eyes for a moment, disguising the movement as a long blink. She waited tensely, but filled with righteous determination, for Reema's response. Her father was examining the fanned pieces of fruit with the air of a man who has heard nothing.

Reema felt as though a badly-honed axe had just slammed down on her fingers. She couldn't believe Tala had just said it like that. Gay. The very word made Reema shudder. It was so far from the reality of marriage and it was miles away from the sexual act, which in its natural state contained within it the image of strong, wild maleness merging thrillingly with willing feminine submission (for on the subject of sex she remained more influenced by her avid reading of romance novels than her own personal experience). Homosexuality sounded like a reckless and disgusting science experiment. Reema felt like screaming.

But the housekeeper had chosen this moment to walk into the room with a fresh pot of mint tea. Carefully, methodically, Rani unloaded the tray, placing the pastries she had brought closer to Tala and reserving to the end the special, gold-filigreed cup, Reema's favourite, which she placed with delicate precision right before her employer. She glanced at Reema and decided against offering her the tea right at that moment, for she was certain she could see the slow grinding of Reema's teeth beneath the muscles that stood out tautly in her jaw. Swiftly, Rani left the room to stand sentinel just outside the door where the acoustics of the conversation inside were best.

Having been forced to swallow her first, instinctual rage (for it would never do to air their dirty – and in this case filthy – laundry in front of the staff) Reema put out her cigarette with a deep sigh of regret, as if the residue of crushed ash contained all her cremated hopes.

'Don't you want to know who it is?' Tala said, looking up, having spent the past minute staring at the floor.

Her mother regarded her balefully.

'It's Leyla,' Tala said, surprised by her own resolve.

In Reema's mind were two considerations. One was that that girl Leyla had always had trouble written all over her face (which, by the way, was the same colour as her numerous staff members) and she cursed herself for not somehow finding a way to remove her from Tala's life. Secondly, and more pertinent to her long-term appraisal of the situation, was the fact that she would have to find a way to cure Tala of this. It was not something one was, it was something one had, and there were ways to get rid of it. Foremost among these was a good marriage, but Tala had obstinately refused to try that method. She wondered briefly about certain camps she had heard of in America, but she didn't know where they were.

'Don't tell a soul,' Reema said. 'Until we sort this out.'

'I'll tell whoever I like. And there's nothing to sort out.'

'Haven't you shamed us enough already?' Reema cried after her daughter, for Tala had gotten up to leave the room. 'You're a disgrace! An aberration!' she yelled, and Tala had time to exchange one, tearful glance with her father before she walked out and slammed the door behind her. Caught between two camps, Omar put a calming hand on Reema's shoulder, but when it became evident that his wife was completely unaware of his presence, he hurried out after his daughter.

In the stillness of the hallway, after the hysterics and the banging of doors had ceased, Rani sensed that her employer might be in need of her. Into the dining room she glided, economical and quiet in her movements, and watched Reema, who was sitting heavily in her chair, one hand on her chest, the other holding listlessly onto her cigarette holder. With great care she poured a cup of warm mint tea for Reema, and offered to her the vessel, where the slick spittle that she had deposited earlier floated unobtrusively, and for the first time since Rani had begun her solitary game, Reema drank.

Chapter 17

MAYA SAT IN THE AUDIENCE bursting with pride while trying to discreetly communicate a signal to Leyla, who was on display amongst all these intellectual people, to sit up straight. But Leyla was not looking at her, she seemed nervous, and who could blame her? The publication of her book was a big event. Maya fought for elbow space with her expansive husband who was taking up the seat to her left and half of her seat besides, and considered how proud she was that she had given birth to a daughter clever enough to write a whole novel. Glowing, she turned to her right to give even her youngest daughter a broad smile of approval. Although she longed for the day when Yasmin would stop throwing live lobsters into her good cooking pots and make something normal for dinner, like a nice chicken tikka or a shepherd's pie, she considered it a coup that at least the child could cook. She caught the outline of Ali's profile, for he sat next to Yasmin (the result of careful manoeuvering on Maya's part) and she noticed how lovely the two of them looked together. And now they were exchanging a glance and a smile as they watched Leyla stand up and begin reading. Maya sighed with pleasure and looked around. In this majestic London courtyard, built of old stones that caught the last autumn rays of the evening sun, she felt happy.

Leyla began her reading with a stomach that felt as if it was filled with rocks and a voice that quavered just slightly, but she tried to focus on the words, tried to remember she was telling a story, and as she became absorbed into that world, she felt her voice relax, and her shoulders too. She rounded off the excerpt elegantly after ten minutes and blushed as everyone applauded. In the audience, which contained more people than she had dared hope to expect, she caught sight of her parents, beaming, and of Yasmin and Ali, clapping still. It was a golden moment, for the sun still sat high enough to coat them, she could feel the touch of it painting her arms. She would have wished for only one more thing to complete her happiness, but that was something and someone that could never be forced and she would learn to accept that fact, somehow, one of these days.

The reading ended and Leyla was led to a small table where she could sign books. Filled with horror at the idea of sitting there and being approached for a signature only by her family, she was greatly relieved to see that a significant queue was forming, and she sat down with her pen, and tried to look casual, as if she did this every day. Out of the corner of one eye, she saw Ali smiling at her, caught a glimpse of her father proudly buying a big stack of her books, and her mother chatting with random audience members, explaining that the famous writer was her daughter. She looked up to find a book being placed before her.

'Can you sign it "Jane Austen"?' Yasmin asked.

Leyla smiled, signed it as herself and looked up as Yasmin moved smartly out of the way for the next person in the queue. After about five minutes, Leyla got into a rhythm, opening the book to the right page and asking who she should sign it for before handing it back with a smile and a few words of conversation.

'Who should I make it out to?' she asked for perhaps the twentieth time in ten minutes. She was thrilled that so many people had waited to buy books. The publisher had told her to keep her expectations low for she was a new writer and nobody would have heard of her.

'To Tala,' came the reply.

Leyla looked up and stared and all sound and sense seemed to drain away. Tala's intent brown eyes held her look for a long moment, until Leyla became aware that she had not breathed for too long, and that she had adopted the attitude of an inelegant statue, mouth slightly open and pen suspended in mid air.

'To Tala,' Tala repeated softly, dictating carefully. 'Who finally had the courage to come out to her parents.'

She replied to Leyla's look of query with a nod and a quiet smile. Clearing her throat, although she could think of nothing rational to say, Leyla looked down at the book. Quickly, she inscribed something inside, closed it and handed it back to Tala. The tips of their fingers touched lightly in the exchange, and Leyla felt the current of it run through her spine.

'Thank you,' Tala said and she moved away.

As soon as she could, Tala stopped, held the book in her palm and looked at it. She smiled with pride to see Leyla's name imprinted on the cover, and then she smiled with embarrassment to note how shaky her own hands were. She took a breath and gently pulled back the front cover to see that Leyla had written only three, short words, but they were the only words she would have wanted to see. Words which Tala had read a thousand times before, in books and also in occasional love letters, but which touched her now as if they had been written down and committed to paper for the first time in history and for her alone.

The sweetness of the moment was broken, but not unhappily, by a hug from Ali, and an introduction to Leyla's sister, a lanky girl whose eyes held a latent sparkle. And those two older people who were approaching them, Tala realized with misgiving, must be Leyla's parents. She resisted the urge to hyperventilate and tried to smile nonchalantly as they said hello. They might know that Leyla was gay, but they certainly didn't need to know that she had ever kissed their daughter, or touched her, or even looked at her. Did they?

'Are you okay, Tala?' Ali touched her arm, and Tala felt the blood rush back to her face.

'Fine, thank you.'

She shook hands with the parents. Leyla's father seemed very nice and offered her another book from a pile he was holding, and her mother was polite too, although the way that she wouldn't meet her eyes, combined with Yasmin's slight smirk made Tala suspect that they all knew exactly what she had done to their daughter once in a hotel room in Oxford. She swallowed hard and looked around to find Leyla coming to join them, finished with the signing. With relief and yet trepidation, Tala moved aside to allow Leyla into the circle, and watched gratefully as attention diverted from herself to the celebrated writer who underwent hugs and kisses from everyone in turn, until she faced Tala and it was Tala's turn to offer congratulations.

Panicked in front of the watching parents, Tala stuck out a hand. She stared at her own fingers, held out in a gesture of formality she had only ever offered to business associates or complete strangers before now. She knew she had to take it back, the hand, and behave like a normal person, like a normal friend, just offer a hug or something, but it was too late. Leyla took the hand and shook it solemnly. Tala's mind rushed back to a first meeting so long ago (and yet not that long, she realized) in her house. Then, slowly, sinuously, she felt Leyla lean forward and Tala could feel her lips brush her cheek very softly, felt her head reeling from the scent of Leyla's skin.

'Sorry to break your reserve,' Leyla said. 'But I don't think a kiss of congratulations is too much to ask?'

Tala nodded and smiled and completed the kiss, but the touch of Leyla's hand on hers, the caress of her clothes against her own was a kind of torture, for she longed to kiss her properly now, to put her lips against hers, to place her hands under her shirt and…

'You must join us for dinner,' Sam said, kindly.

Inwardly, imperceptibly, Tala shook herself and tried not to appear breathless.

'I'd love to,' she said, because she could not be away from Leyla, but she wondered how she could make it through a whole meal without betraying herself. And what would happen afterwards?

'Booked you a hotel room,' Yasmin said to them under her breath as they finally left the restaurant and stood about on the pavement. 'Happy Christmas.'

'Christmas is three months away,' Leyla said.

'Yeah, well, don't expect anything under the tree,' clarified Yasmin with a grin. She scribbled a hotel name on the back of a napkin and handed it over.

'Come on, Mum and Dad,' Yasmin said, hailing a taxi. 'Ali and I will get you home. These two are going out to celebrate.'

'Now?' exclaimed Maya. 'But it's ten o'clock already.'

'Mum, they're not eighty,' said Yasmin, and Maya's retort was lost as she was bundled unceremoniously into the back of the cab. With a final glance back at Leyla and Tala, and a look that was not without a wistful regret, Ali joined the others in the taxi and waved from the window.

The slam of the door opening back against the wall echoed down the plush corridors of the hotel but Leyla didn't notice, for Tala's mouth was on hers as they fell into the room. Closing the door with her foot, she leaned back against the wall, tasting Tala's tongue chasing her own, pulling off Tala's jacket. Tala's mouth moved down to her neck, following the line of her fingers which were undoing the buttons of Leyla's shirt, fumbling urgently, releasing finally the swollen breasts and kissing them, licking, caressing the erect nipples with a tongue that was gentle but insistent. Leyla reached down, her hands slipping inside Tala's bra, then moving down, stroking her stomach, reaching for her belt, pulling it open, sliding her hand inside her panties, but Tala slipped down further, onto her knees and out of reach, her tongue tracing a line down Leyla's abdomen and down further, lowering her trousers with hands that lingered over her and spread open the legs that could barely keep Leyla upright.

Leyla moaned, her head falling back at the play of that tongue touching her; there was no thought, no feeling, nothing except the waves of sensation, her hips moving against Tala's mouth until she cried out. Shaking, she slid down on top of Tala, who held her close against her own skin, their bodies fused together so that, in the indefinable world revealed by her heightened senses, Leyla could not tell where hers ended and Tala's began.

In an expensive restaurant in Amman, amid the excitable chatter of lunchtime diners, Hani sat with Reema, newly arrived from London, and tried to make conversation that did not touch on politics, religion or sexuality. The first two were never easy to avoid in the Middle East, and the last topic was foremost in both their minds because of Tala. Hani tried another bite of flatbread with thyme, and momentarily regretted having invited his near mother-in-law to lunch. He had done so because he knew he was the only one who could try to talk to her about Tala, and because it would not hurt for Amman society to see that he bore no hard feelings towards Tala's family for what had happened. But here they sat, ten minutes into the meal and already they had exhausted the weather, the plane ride and his work as items of discussion.

'Aunty?' Hani said suddenly. 'About Tala. It's not the end of the world.'

A burst of laughter, unconnected but cruelly timed burst up from the table behind them, hidden from view by discreet banquettes and potted plants. Reema sighed and picked up a cigarette. Hani leaned over, lighter ready.

'As long as she's happy, Aunty,' he tried again. 'That's what really matters.'

Reema regarded him without enthusiasm. Perhaps it was a good thing Tala hadn't married him. The boy was clearly a crackpot.

'Happiness is not the issue,' she explained, slowly, as if to someone of limited mental faculty. 'People will talk,' she hissed.

'You know what? No-one knows. And if they find out, I don't think they'll even care. Times have changed, Aunty. Even here.'

Again the laughter from the table nearby, but this time, in the silence that Reema imposed with a withering look at Hani, they caught a snatch of the conversation between four women:

'No, come on!'

'She's what?'

'You're joking, habibti! Tala?!'

Hani squirmed as the other women quieted their friend down. The gossip continued, with low undertones passing back to Reema, who had assumed the rigid mien of a stone carving.

'I have to say,' said one of the women, in a tone that carried. 'I don't see what all the fuss is. About Tala.'

Hani breathed. This was promising. Could he allow a smile?

'I mean,' she continued. 'Some of my best friends are Lebanese.'

Closing his eyes for just a moment, Hani found that he could.

THE END

Director Shamim Sarif on the set of I Can't Think Straight

Sheetal Sheth ('Leyla') and Antonia Frering ('Reema') share a joke on set

Shamim Sarif sets up a shot

Shamim Sarif & Sheetal Sheth ('Leyla') between shots on location in Battersea Park

Lisa Ray ('Tala'), Sheetal Sheth and Shamim discuss the Jordan lecture sequence

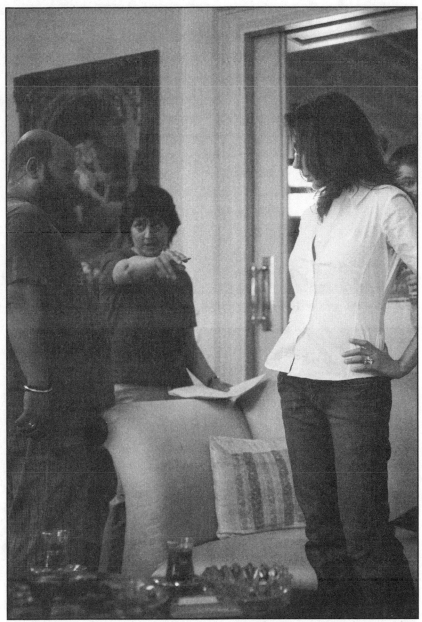

Lisa Ray waits as Shamim Sarif and cinematographer Aseem Bajaj discuss a shot

Lisa Ray and Shamim Sarif between shots. On the far right is Daud Shah ('Hani')

Producer Hanan Kattan and director Shamim Sarif in a quiet moment on set